THREE HOURS PAST MIDNIGHT

Tony Knighton

Three Hours Past Midnight

Crime Wave Press
Flat D, 11th Fl. Liberty Mansion
26E Jordan Road
Yau Ma Tei, Hong Kong
www.crimewavepress.com

ISBN 978-988-14938-5-9

Cover photo: Peter Rozovsky.

"With a classic heist goes wrong set up, Tony Knighton takes us on a violent, danger-strewn tour through the night time streets of Philadelphia. Everyone has an angle, no one gives an inch. Fans of David Goodis and Richard Stark should love this one."

— Scott Adlerberg, author of *Graveyard Love*

Three Hours Past Midnight is a night prowler's blitz tour of Philadelphia, boiled hard and served straight up. Damn. Burnt my fingertips, blistered my eyeballs and I want to go again."

- Jedidian Ayres, author of *Peckerwood*

"A pitch-perfect tale of crime and consequences. Just try and put it down before the last page. I dare you."

— Charles Ardai Editor, Hard Case Crime

Other books by Tony Knighton published by Crime Wave Press:
Happy Hour and Other Philadelphia Cruelties

For Julie Odell

1

When the girl got out of the car across the intersection, George said, "Won't be long now." He adjusted the rear view mirror to follow her progress. The back of his hand was bruised; the vestiges of IV line tape there described an X. Even with the windows down, his car smelled of cigarette smoke. A tune played quietly over the radio. George liked music.

I turned in the passenger seat and watched the girl walk away. She was young, probably just off the boat from some Asian shit hole. A breeze gently tossed her hair, and the leaves of the magnolia trees that lined the sidewalk. The cop came out of the unmarked car's back seat while fixing his pants. He got back in behind the wheel.

George took off his glasses and cleaned the thick lenses with a handkerchief. He said, "It's been the same the last couple nights. His sergeant comes by around six-thirty or seven to check on him. After that, he orders himself up a blowjob from Lucky Number and falls asleep. He must set his phone to wake him before his relief shows." George replaced his glasses and stifled a cough. "Nobody any good wants to be stuck on something like this. That guy," he nodded in the direction of the plainclothesman, "never was a ball of fire." I watched the cop. He settled in, leaning back against the headrest.

I turned around. George coughed and spit into the handkerchief, and absently inspected the result. As he stuffed the cloth in his hip pocket he glanced at me and said, "Sorry."

A few cars came up the street, slowly, the drivers searching for parking. The neighborhood was high-end, but also high-density residential, nestled between the Parkway and Fairmount Avenue, and there were restaurants and a club scene nearby, so parking was tight. One car, a Mercedes, slowed to a stop and its driver stared at us, annoyed. George said, "Guy probably thinks we're queer." His chuckle ended in a wheeze. The Mercedes continued around the corner.

The tune on the radio ended. The announcer said, "That was Lee Morgan playing McCoy Tyner's *Twilight Mist.* It's a breezy eighty-nine degrees here at WRTI studios on the Temple University campus in North Philadelphia, with the possibility of a late evening thunder storm. In local news, a house fire in the Olney section of the city has traffic on the Roosevelt Boulevard snarled. A second unidentified woman's body was discovered on the banks of the Delaware River in Tinicum Township this afternoon. A spokesperson for SEPTA now says that earlier estimates for returning its rail fleet to full operation may have been overly optimistic – "

George lowered the volume and punched the lighter on the dash. Pointing a thumb over his shoulder toward the cop, he said, "He's nodding already." George unwound a power cord and stuck a cigarette in his mouth. When the lighter popped out, he lit up and produced a thin metal box from under his seat, and used the cord to connect it to the lighter receptacle. George had explained its operation to me earlier: "The security system connects to the alarm company through the same cell towers your phone uses. This," he'd held up the box, "is like a rogue base station – essentially a mini cell tower. It doesn't have enough power to work at any distance, but right across the street it'll work fine. The security system will seek this instead of the cell tower and route all its signals to the inside of my car, and that's where they'll stay. You could start World War Three in that house and nobody would know."

I flexed my fingers inside my gloves. George took another drag and went into a coughing fit. His face turned red and he dropped the cigarette to the floorboard between his feet. He struggled to catch his breath. I said, "Are you going to be able to do this?"

George put a hand on my forearm and was nodding yes before he got himself under control. His grip tightened, as though to keep me from leaving him, and when he was able, he said, "Yeah. Yeah, I got it." He recovered the cigarette and threw it out the window. "I know. It's horrible. I gotta quit these things." I stared at him. George said, "I'm okay." He looked up at the rear view again and said, "It's cool. Go ahead." He took his handkerchief again and wiped his eyes.

My last outing had been three months before, and hadn't gone well. I needed this. I got out of the car. George had removed the bulb from the ceiling lamp. I appreciated his attention to detail. Sick or not, George was a pro.

I took a gym bag from the trunk and walked across the street to the property. The house was a huge three-story single, an Italianate brownstone with lots of detail in the masonry. Even here, in a neighborhood of big twins and townhouses, it stood out.

Its front yard's shoulder high wall was built of the same cut stone as the house. In the twilight, it looked almost purple. I climbed the terraced, flagstone walkway to the front door. The key the woman had given George turned stiffly in the lock but worked. I ignored the alarm keypad on the wall in the vestibule. The woman knew the code from a few months before, but we had no way to know if Pastore had changed it in the interim. That was why we were using George's gizmo.

Even in the dim light, it was apparent that this was a rich man's home. Fine oriental rugs covered the traveled areas in the hallway. It was trimmed in dark woodwork – wainscoting and crown molding. In the rooms flanking the hallway, the windows extended from the hardwood floors almost to the fourteen-foot ceilings. The furnishings sounded a wrong note – they were expensive but didn't fit – a lot of chrome and brass and blonde wood. A golf bag full of Ping irons and Callaway woods sat in the hallway next to the mail table, as though Pastore would be coming home like nothing had happened.

Lining the hallway and stairs were awards, and dozens of framed photographs of important people, and Pastore was with them in every picture – smiling, shaking hands, cutting ribbons. One was of him and a bunch of suits at a groundbreaking, all wearing hard hats; Pastore smiled on as the mayor plunged the shovel. Another photo was of him receiving an award in front of a banner that read "Chinese-American Businessman's Association." Several more were photos of Pastore and others on a large, sport-fishing boat. In one, the legend, "Mover 'n Shaker" decorated the stern. In a lot of the photos, a slight, rat-faced man stood next to Pastore, or at least nearby. In all of them, if there were more than one person other than himself, Pastore insinuated himself between them, most likely to prevent photo editors from cropping him out. I got the sense that these pictures were on display primarily to impress his visitors, much like the family portrait on a car salesman's desk was turned toward and for the benefit of the customers.

At the landing was a flattering likeness of the man in oils. In it he wore a dark three-piece suit and seemed to be thinner than he was. His hair was thicker. He appeared contemplative.

I climbed the rest of the way to the second floor. The railing alone would cost tens of thousands to replace. A smoke alarm was mounted on the wall in the hallway. It would sound inside the house. There was going to be a lot of dust. I stood on a chair, wrapped a plastic shopping bag around the alarm and cinched it with a rubber band.

I went straight to the closet in the master bedroom and began grabbing up everything on hangers and throwing it all on the big, four-poster bed. Pastore had a lot of clothes – suits, mostly dark, mostly single-breasted, with vertical stripes. Lots of oxford-cloth shirts with French cuffs. It took me four armfuls to empty the closet, along with a DVR camera and tripod, and a trombone case, and I removed the clothes rod and shelf. I needed the room to work.

The safe was mounted on the far left-side wall of the closet, away from the light. It was about fifteen by twenty-four inches square, with a gray steel face. A combination dial was set in the front.

I took coveralls and a painter's hat from the gym bag, and a dust mask and goggles and put them all on, and attacked the wall surrounding the safe with a hatchet and pry-bar, chopping at it until there was a ragged swath cut around the safe's perimeter. I was ankle deep in debris – plaster and bits of lathe. Even with the mask, I was choking on the dust.

The safe was bolted to the partition studs – two by sixes. I cut them with a cordless Sawzall, below and above, and yanked the safe free of the opening. Lathe and plaster from the adjoining room came along with it. The safe was about four inches deep, and heavy, sixty or seventy pounds. I tapped it on its back – solid. Getting it open would be no joke.

I stripped off the coveralls, gathered up the tools and put them all in the gym bag. When I had everything together, I slid open a window on the Twenty-second Street side of the house. George saw me and got out of the car, and checked the intersection. He let a couple cars go by and nodded. I muscled the safe up onto the sill and pushed. It landed in the grass with a *thunk.* I tossed the gym bag next to it.

George was struggling with the safe as I slid shut the window. As I wiped the dust off my face with one of Pastore's shirts, George dragged the safe to the car. I saw him hoist it over the bumper and drop it into the trunk. The car rocked on its springs. He leaned on the fender and caught his breath, and went back for the gym bag. Two cars went by. I didn't like it; George was calling attention to himself. He finally got back into the car and took off.

I went downstairs and out the door. My shoulder hurt. Another car was already backing into the spot George had vacated. On my way out to Spring Garden Street, I looked over at the cop. He was still asleep.

2

A day earlier, I'd met George for coffee. I hadn't seen him in over a year. He'd lost a lot of weight. He said, "I heard you got hurt."

I was quiet for a few seconds, and said, "Who told you that?"

"Oh, I don't know. You forget where you hear things." George fiddled with a packet of sugar. "Around, somewhere, you know?"

"Yeah. Broken collarbone." I rotated my left shoulder. It hurt. "I'm all right now."

"Good." George nodded and said, "Shame about Redfern."

"Who's that?"

"Really?" His expression showed amusement.

I didn't answer him.

He hesitated and said, "A guy like us. I heard he got shot on a job out near Harrisburg."

I didn't know if George was just showing me that he'd kept up with things or if this was something else. Either way I didn't like it. He should know better. I got up and sat next to him on his side of the booth. George leaned away and said, "What?" Without saying anything, I put my hand on his chest and felt for anything that might be under his shirt. He was startled and said, "Whoa, what are you doing?" Then he got it and relaxed a little. "Oh. Hey, look, you don't have to – I wouldn't –" He coughed and covered his mouth.

I said, "Calm down." George felt frail. I couldn't feel anything like a wire or recording device. There was a pen in his shirt pocket. I took it out. It looked expensive. I dropped it on the floor and cracked it under my heel. "Everyone needs to be careful. Especially you." I dumped the ramekin of sugar packets on the tabletop and went through them, put them all onto the next table, and continued, "Be very careful about how you explain why you wanted to talk to me." I popped open the napkin dispenser and thumbed my way through the tissues. A woman working at her computer two tables over looked up and stared for a moment. When she saw that I was watching her, she looked away.

George glanced down at the ruined pen but said, "I get it. Careful." I stared at him. He sensed my impatience and said, "Tom said that you were looking for work. If so, I got something. I know you don't like to do things close to home but I think this is worth it."

I waited. Up close, George looked waxy. His pale skin was stretched tight across his face. He continued, "Yeah, you never were one for small talk. You heard of Vic Pastore?"

"State legislator or something?"

George nodded. "State senator."

"Did I hear he's having some trouble?"

"Yeah, you could say that. Last August he got indicted on a bribery charge. The State's Attorney General had been looking into his finances for a couple of years. They convened a grand jury. Pastore held a news conference and laughed it off. He said it was political – just a bunch of hicks from the middle of the state that don't like people from Philadelphia. He said, 'a grand jury could indict a ham sandwich.'"

George let me mull that over and continued, "It turns out the Feds were looking at him, too. They've gotten together with guys from the city and the state. They formed a joint-task force, dedicated to investigating Pastore and his dealings. It's all supposed to be very hush-hush, but you know cops—"

"Yeah, they can't keep their mouths shut."

George winced, and said, "Look, that thing about Redfern, I'm sorry."

"Okay."

"Can you move back to your side of the table now? So we can talk like normal people do, please?" He took a handful of napkins and coughed into them.

I did, and said. "Go on."

George leaned forward, his arms on the tabletop. "They grabbed Pastore yesterday. Took him out of his office here in the city. In cuffs. He's being held at the Federal Detention Center on Arch Street. His lawyers are arguing for bail, but the US Attorney is claiming that he's a flight risk, and so far a Third District judge is listening to him."

"Isn't that extreme?"

"That's what his lawyer's arguing, but the judge is standing firm. I heard from a friend they're going to charge him with violations of the RICO statute."

"What for?"

"They say he's defrauded everybody – charities, non-profits – anybody that went through him to get any kind of government or non-government grant. They're going over all his real estate deals. The list just goes on and on. He took a bite out of everything. And he didn't do it by himself. They want to charge him with being part of a continuing criminal enterprise. Conspiracy, the works. They want to roll up everybody in his organization and beyond." George reached to his shirt pocket for a cigarette and remembered himself. "The beauty part of this move is that he didn't know what they had planned."

"What else?"

"They wanted to swoop in and grab his assets. Publicly – reporters, TV, everything. He wouldn't have the chance to hide the stuff that he hadn't already hidden."

"What would that be?"

"Something in his house. Place was his dad's. It's still in his mother's name even though she's down in Florida. None of that matters. They already have the warrants. They were gonna go in yesterday when they locked him up, but that thing with the SEPTA rail cars happened, and they're holding off for better media coverage. They want the front page." George smiled.

I knew what George meant – a circus. Two seconds after forcing the door, they'd be setting up the folding tables out front to display seized items for the cameras, and a podium for police brass and prosecutors to make speeches congratulating themselves.

I didn't need all of this background, but George liked to talk, so I listened. Eventually, he'd get to it. He went on, "They had all this – the bust, the seizure – re-scheduled for a couple days from now. It was all under wraps until they tried to subpoena Pastore's chief of staff, this guy Ed Reilly. Little weasely guy, been with Pastore for years. He's disappeared. That's why the Task-Force needed to move in quickly, before Pastore or anybody else tried to get out of Dodge."

George said, "Anyway, there's this woman, used to date Pastore. She says he stole way more than anybody knows. Says that Vic has a close to half a million in a safe in the house. Cash."

"Get out."

"No, this is solid."

"Who is this woman?"

"She's originally from the neighborhood – downtown. Now she lives in Center City. Works for a law firm –"

"She a lawyer?"

"No – secretary. They met at a fundraiser. Apparently, he likes blondes. She went out with him for a while. They broke up a few months ago."

"How does she know that he has all this money?"

"He likes to play the big shot. Always likes to flash a big wad, pay for everything with cash. He used to brag to her all the time about money that nobody knew he had – the state, the IRS, nobody."

"That's just talk."

"She saw it. She saw him open a safe in his bedroom closet and take out a wad."

"Then he'll know it was her. She'll fold up in five minutes." George was talking himself into something that wasn't worth the trouble. I added, "I don't like a job with somebody on the inside."

George shook his head. "I said that to her. He never knew she saw it. That's the beauty of this. She came back into the bedroom while the tub was filling. He was busy in the closet. She saw stacks of bills this high." He held his hand six inches off the table. "He took out a wad and pulled an inch worth of bills off it. All hundreds. She went back into the bathroom before he turned around." George coughed and wiped his mouth with a handkerchief, and said, "This is a smart girl. He'd given her a key to his house after they'd been dating a little while. She knew it wasn't going to last and made a copy for herself. So that's our way in. I can handle the alarm."

This woman was a tease. Telling George about the bath was inviting him to imagine her naked, but I let that go for the time being. Dating for "a little while" seemed unusual for sharing keys. I let that go, too. Instead, I said, "Why did she wait so long?"

"To have enough of a buffer, enough time. They break up and he gets robbed two weeks later, he thinks about her. This way, he doesn't." He moved his hand over the table, palm down, as though erasing the man's memory. "She was going to wait longer, but then all this happened."

"He might not have it there now. Or at all."

"Where else would he put it? I still think it's worth going for." He smiled and said, "So do you. You're still listening."

I ignored that and said, "How did she find you?"

"Through a lawyer I know." George anticipated my next question and shook his head. "Nobody that she works with – a neighborhood guy. We've helped each other out with some things."

I mulled that over and said, "What do they want?"

"Just a finder's fee. Fifteen per cent of whatever we take. I think she wanted more, but this guy convinced her we'd be more likely to play fair if she didn't ask for too much."

"Who else knows about this?"

"Pastore's trouble? Anybody that watches the news."

"I mean the money."

"Nobody. They came to me and me only."

I wasn't sure about that, but if I waited for something perfect, I'd wait forever. There were other things to go over. "Somebody's going to be watching that place until they go inside."

"You're right, they are, but I've got it covered."

"How?"

"Something like this, it all comes down to budgets and turf." George settled in, clearly in his element; he liked explaining things. I could easily picture him in front of a class of college freshmen. "Twenty-four hour a day surveillance costs money. Between the feds, the state and the city, a lot of police agencies are involved in this thing. They all want to take credit for the bust and seizure, but none of them want to pay for it. The city agreed to handle surveillance in exchange for certain promises. See, twenty years ago, Philadelphia was in the red, and Pastore was instrumental in setting up state oversight of city contracts. Fucked all the new hires. Some of those guys he fucked have rank now, and they have long memories. They want payback." He smiled. "It just so happens I know the guy that ended up stuck with the four to midnight watch."

I said, "Another friend?" This was turning into too many people. "Somebody else we have to cut in?"

"No." George smiled again. "Not at all."

"Why not?"

"You gotta realize, the best guys never get stuck on this kind of job. It's shit work. Believe me, I have it covered."

"This all sounds complicated."

"Not our end. We're just taking something out of a house."

I stared at George and said, "Who did you ask in on this before me?"

"What do you mean?"

"Come on, George. We're not that close. Who did you call first?"

"Look," George licked his lips and said, "Look, I did try one other guy, but he didn't even listen. He has something going on, something else. Out on the coast, somewhere. He didn't want to hear anything about it, this thing, here." George played with his cigarettes. "Before they grabbed Pastore, I'd been working out a whole different approach to this – using a van with a commercial cleaner's name and number on the side, going in with a cart in the middle of the day – nobody else in on it, just me, but that won't work now, with Pastore in jail and the surveillance and all. I just asked this other guy if he was available, nothing else."

George probably told the other guy more than that, but not enough to be a problem. He saw that I was unconvinced and added, "I only mentioned to Tom that I needed some help with something. He told me you were looking. That's all."

I said, "That's okay." George looked relieved, and I said, "What about the guy you heard about Pastore's legal troubles from?"

George looked confused for a moment and said, "My friend is not like us."

"He told you. He could tell someone else."

"Not likely. Trust me. This is just me and you."

"Can the two of us handle this?"

"Yes."

"Ok." That was good. I was leery of jobs that needed a lot of hands – too many personalities to deal with, too many people who needed to be trusted.

I doubted there were half a million dollars, but figured that if there were even a fraction of that, it could be worth it. The task-force thing bothered me, though. There was a lot of manpower there. If one person knows something, it's a secret. If they tell someone else, it isn't anymore. George was right; cops can't keep their mouths shut. If he found out, how many others might know about this?

I stared at George while I thought. His clothes hung loose on him. I said, "What's wrong with you?"

He gave me a weak grin and said, "I was wondering when you were gonna get around to that." He tapped his chest. "I'm stage four."

"Then why are you doing this?"

"Money. What else?"

"I wouldn't like it if you're looking for kicks, some kind of last hurrah—"

"No, nothing like that. My pension from the department doesn't go very far. I want to leave my wife some money." He tried to smile and said, "I never gave Jeanie much of a life. I want to try to make all this worth something to her." George stared down at the table, lost in his thoughts, and became self-conscious and looked up at me. He sensed that I wasn't convinced, and said, "This is business. I'll hold up my end."

"All right." George relaxed a little. I said, "The timing is tricky. They'll know that somebody went in ahead of them."

"Yeah, but that's okay. They'll look at Pastore's people first, and then all the guys in the task force will be suspect. It'll be a long time before anybody gets around to looking at guys like us."

I thought a little more and said, "They're going to want to go in soon."

"Yup. Day after tomorrow." He fingered his cigarettes again and said, "I already started last night, watching the watcher. I'll watch him tonight, too. We hit it tomorrow night."

George was selling this too hard. I didn't like to work this close to home. It was bad policy. If I had trouble here, it could ruin everything I'd built up over the years – my house, my straight-arrow persona, and my straight-arrow life. I didn't like the timing either. I like more time to look things over and think about it. Plus, George fooled around more than I cared for. I hadn't liked his crack about Redfern. George should know better.

As if he'd read my mind, he said, "Look, that thing I said, about Redfern – "

"I said it was okay."

"No, what I mean is, well, that job out there didn't go well."

I waited, and George said, "Please don't misunderstand me, I know you're a professional. Other guys, though, they might wonder."

"Wonder what?"

"Whether or not you let Reds down." All the worry was gone from his face.

I said, "The police killed him."

George said, "That's what the papers said, anyway."

"That's what happened."

"Funny how none of the money was recovered."

I said, "You never met any cops who stole things?"

"Touché." George touched his fingertips to his forehead but added, "Redfern had a lot of friends."

"Professionals don't make threats, George."

His expression softened, and he said, "Come on, this is no threat. It's a nice offer. Let's do this and get well."

I still didn't like it, but George was smart, and he was right. He knew how to make a plan, and on a job he was solid. I was running low on cash. Mostly, though, my last job had gone bad. I needed to get back on the horse.

I said, "Okay."

And the next night I chopped the safe out of the wall and dropped it out the window.

3

George's shop was on the north side of Callowhill Street, in a four-story building in a row of neglected mercantile properties just like it, along the idled Reading Viaduct. George didn't need a fancy storefront to run his straight business. The neighborhood was mostly dead by this time of night. This had been the old Tenderloin, where the Center City cops had herded and corralled the stew bums, back before society changed and bums became 'the homeless.' There were still shelters nearby.

I cabbed to a corner on Vine Street, a block shy of George's place, paid the driver and walked north. I heard music in the distance. A couple cars went by. Up ahead, a hipster couple pedaled hard around the corner in my direction, bucking traffic. The kid was dressed too warmly for the weather – a knit cap and flannel shirt, but the girl wore a tank top that showed off her tattoos – some kind of vine that curled around and over her arms and upper chest. She had long black hair cut like Betty Paige, and wore those glasses that ladies used to wear, the kind with pointed corners that look like cat's eyes.

A red Ford Econoline with Jersey tags rocked to a stop at the end of George's block, despite having the green light. A streetlight on the van's far side silhouetted its driver. He looked in my direction and reached down for something on the floor. I stopped short; this was a bad spot. I looked for cover – nothing. Around the corner sounded the *whoop* of a siren as a cop tweaked its signal. The van driver glanced at his side-view mirror and back in my direction, and drove through the intersection. A second later, a patrol car turned north, away from me.

I didn't like it. I picked up the pace. A punk band down the street was going through the motions, practicing a tune in one of the properties. In this neighborhood they didn't have to watch the volume.

I banged on George's roll-up garage door and waited. When there wasn't an answer the second time, I went around the corner and down the narrow street between the row of buildings and the viaduct wall. The music sounded louder back here.

The inside of George's building was dark. I wiped dirt off the window with the side of my hand and shone my penlight through the glass. His car was visible inside, the trunk lid open. George was slumped over the wheel.

I looked around the street. Two buildings away, a mossy cinder block served as a step up to the back door. I knocked the glass out of a bottom pane with it, unlocked and raised the sash, and boosted myself over the sill. The place smelled of dry rot and soldering flux. The benches were full with circuitry and components. A Fender amp chassis sat upside-down on a work surface, its tubes loose on a doubled up towel.

The trunk was empty. I pressed two fingers to the side of George's neck; there was no pulse, and no point in dragging him outside and calling 911. I pushed him up in the seat. Looking closely, I could see a small dark spot in the center of George's sports shirt, surrounded by scorch marks and a little blood. He'd been shot at close range.

I heard a car turn into the back street and saw red lights streak across the window. The guy in the van had shot George, seen me on the street and called the police.

I took the stairs two at a time. As I gained the fourth flight, I heard footsteps and voices inside. I went all the way up and climbed the ladder to the roof hatch and outside. Two more squad cars turned onto the street.

Three doors down was a building with apartments on its upper floors and a metal fire escape bolted to its back face. I ran down a flight, stepped over the railing and jumped from the third floor across the gap to the viaduct, landed and rolled. It knocked the wind out of me, and for a moment I worried I might have re-broken my shoulder, but got to my feet and ran. The punk band played on, oblivious. One of the cops in the alley saw me go overhead, and shouted, "He's up on the tracks." Another, on the roof, tried to trace my path with the beam of his Maglight but lost me in the ghetto palms and creepers that grew up through the rails and fouled the catenary. None of the officers followed me across the gap. They weren't risking a broken ankle for cop's pay.

The abandoned railway cut through the grid of streets diagonally, making it difficult for them to give chase by car. I ran a few blocks north. The going was hard, running through the ballast between the tracks. I hopped down onto the roof of an adjacent one-story building, dropped to the street and climbed up and into the empty bed of a dump truck. A few seconds later I heard a car speed by, but then nothing.

I waited another minute, and stuck my head up, and not seeing anything, hopped out and kept moving north. While I walked, I thought about my choices: this had gone bad, but I was out of it if I wanted to be. The police had nothing – they hadn't gotten a good look at me, they had no prints, and no idea who I was. I could go home and forget about this.

That left me right where I was before George had called – looking for a score. The guy in the red van had my safe and my money. Was he the other guy George had called, or was this something else? I didn't know where the trouble had come from, or who else was in this. Would someone be happier to have me dead? The more I thought about it the less I liked it.

More than that, George's point had been well made: guys in the life would wonder about Redfern. Now George was dead, in the middle of doing a job with me. I had to do something about that – something loud. I had to run this down. I needed a gun.

4

I got the passenger door of a yellow Plymouth opened and popped the hood, put the picks in my wallet and sprawled across the doorstep of a vacant building thirty feet away. On the other side of the street was a one-story commercial property, painted blue, with a sign over the door that read "Colosimo's: Guns & Ammo – Target Range." Business hours were long over but it was still open in the evening to members. Even with soundproofing, the gunfire inside was audible. A lot of SUV's were parked in the little street. Most of them had an NRA decal fixed to the back window. I could watch the range's front door through a gap between two parked cars. My clothes were dirty from my run along the viaduct. Anyone happening by would assume that I was drunk or homeless, or both.

The first couple guys who exited the range looked too much like cops – short hair and bad mustaches. A white, late model Mazda Miata drove by slowly. Its driver stared at the range. A few minutes later a man in his thirties came out of the building with a black plastic case under his arm – it looked like something made to hold a cordless drill. He fiddled with his keys as he walked toward a Chevy. I called out to him as I approached, "Excuse me, could you give me a jump?' He looked up, startled, but relaxed as I pointed over my shoulder to the Plymouth's open hood. I did my best to look sheepish. "I left my lights on," and added, "I've got a set of cables."

He nodded and turned back to his car, "Sure. Just let me—" I bounced his head off the roof and the fender, opened the trunk and dumped him inside.

I didn't like this; it was unprofessional. The description "non-violent offender" means a lot to law enforcement. Police get more interested when somebody gets hurt, especially if that somebody is a citizen. It couldn't be helped. Because I don't like to work close to home, most of the guys who I get guns from were away from here. There were a couple guys in town whom I'd dealt with before, but I didn't like to. They were both hard to get in touch with. You made a call and left a message. Sometime later, they'd get back to you and you'd work out where to meet. It all took time that I didn't have. There were two other reasons not to call those guys: they'd wonder why I wanted a gun on short notice and maybe decide to deal themselves in. The second reason was that either of them could have been the guy who'd killed George.

I drove to a parking garage on Sixth Street, and put the guy's car up on the fourth level. Inside the case was a target pistol, a Ruger Mark III, chambered for twenty-two long rifles. There was an extra magazine and an open box of cartridges. I'd have preferred something heavier, but it would do. I put it all – the pistol, the magazine and spare rounds – into a plastic shopping bag the guy had in the console and walked down a level to the car I was using, a gray '91 Toyota – a very anonymous vehicle. I put the pistol and rounds under the seat, drove down the ramp and handed the attendant the ticket I'd just gotten, paid and pulled away.

George's house was downtown, on one of the little cul de sacs near the stadiums. There was a police car out front. This was the department's unofficial courtesy call to the wife of a retired officer – this cop would be breaking the news. The hard questions would come later, when the detectives ran out of ideas at the scene. I waited down the street until I saw the cop pull away, and went up and knocked. When his wife answered, I said, "I'm a friend of George. I'd like to talk to you."

She didn't look like she wanted to let me in, but did, and said, "I don't suppose I have to tell you what happened?" She was handling it better than I'd have thought. She'd probably been expecting something like this for years. "Do I?"

I moved into the living room as she closed the door. "No. Who knew what George was doing tonight?"

She said, "You sure don't waste any time, do you?" In the light she looked younger than George, but probably just took better care of herself. She looked taller than him, too. "How would I know? I have no idea what he was up to."

She was lying, but it didn't make sense that the trouble would come from her; if she'd sold us out she'd only have to split with somebody else. I said, "I need to talk to his lawyer."

"Go right ahead." She walked around the little house straightening things that didn't need to be straightened. "Be my guest." It was as though what she'd expected – this moment that she'd rehearsed for all this time – suddenly didn't feel like she'd thought it should.

"I don't know who he is. What's his name?"

She'd been in control until now but let go. "Why should I tell you his name? Why would I tell you anything? Maybe you're the one –"

"I didn't kill him."

She composed herself and said, "It doesn't matter. You'd say that anyway."

"If I'd killed him, I wouldn't be here now. George got waylaid. He was killed being robbed."

"Why didn't they kill you?"

"I was somewhere else when it happened." She was quiet. I said, "If I can get a line on whoever knew about what George was doing, I can find who did it."

"I don't care about that. George was done anyway. He'd have been gone in three months, tops, and honestly, we weren't all that chummy anymore."

"You could have fooled me a minute ago."

She was quiet and spoke more softly. "People drift apart. I stopped loving George, but I didn't want to see him hurt. You spend that much time with anybody, you don't want to see something bad happen to them."

I needed her to focus on the present. "There's money in this if you help me."

"George's share?"

"No. George doesn't have a share anymore. I'll give you a finder's fee."

"How much is that?"

"Ten per cent." She was thinking. I said, "I could lie and say I'll give you more and then never give you anything."

"You could be lying now."

"You're right."

She hesitated a moment and went to an oak cabinet with glass doors in the dining room, and took a business card from an antique cut glass sugar bowl. Next to the bowl sat a green glass perfume bottle and stopper, about the size of a tea cup, covered with decorative silver work. A medallion was engraved with the monogram JDA.

She handed me the card and said, "George didn't have anything saved. His pension from the department isn't much and now I'll only get half."

I ignored all that and said, "Did George know anybody who owns a Ford van with Jersey tags?"

She was tired of answering questions. "I don't know many of George's friends."

I put the card in my pocket and moved toward the door. She said, "Did he. . . ?" She put her hand to her mouth.

I looked at her and said, "It wasn't as bad as what he was looking at," and left.

5

I found a payphone on Broad Street. The lawyer's name was Michael Marcolina. The card showed an office address on Snyder Avenue. There were two phone numbers listed. The first proved to be the man's office. A recorded voice said to leave a message. I called the second number and when a man answered, said, "I'm calling for George." I could hear crowd noises in the background.

He hesitated and said, "George who?"

"George who has business with you." There wasn't a response. "I don't want to go into it over the phone."

He seemed to get it. "Why isn't George calling for himself?"

"He can't."

He was quiet for a moment, and said, "What can I do for you?"

I said, "It's what I can do for you that you'll be interested in."

"Ok. And what would that be?"

"I'd rather not go into it over –"

"Right, right, over the phone." He paused for a moment and said, "I'm not free at the present. Could I meet you somewhere in, let's say," there was another pause, "an hour?"

I wanted to see him sooner, but I couldn't press this. "Sure." If he spooked, he could just hole up somewhere.

He said, "Meet me on Passyunk Avenue by the statue of Joey Giardello. You know where that's at?"

"Yeah."

"Ok. How will I know you?"

"We'll figure it out." I hung up.

I tried to think this through from another direction. It was too much of a stretch to imagine that this was simply a matter of opportunity. Somebody had to know about this job – at least part of it – to have hijacked us.

It was no good trying to run it down from the mechanical end; anyone handy, with access to tools and a shop, or a garage, or even a basement, would be able to open that box in a few hours.

It had sounded like Marcolina was in a bar. I took a ride past his office. It was in a row of two-story properties of first floor businesses – a grocery store, a barber, a dry cleaner – with apartments upstairs. The block had seen its prime come and go.

I circled the block and parked across the street to look things over. There was a good amount of auto traffic but not many people on foot. I got out and crossed the street. The office was dark, but I could make out the interior from the streetlights. There was no sign of an alarm keypad inside the door.

The front door lock was a Kwikset. I had a bump key that I'd cut from a Kwikset blank. The lock turned the second time I tapped the back of the key with the handle of my penknife. Inside, I locked the door and looked through the receptionist's desk drawers. They were empty. Marcolina had no receptionist; the desk was there for show.

The door to the main office was unlocked. There was a desk and swivel chair, two straight-backed chairs facing it, and a file cabinet. The office had one small window, facing the breezeway. On the wall behind the desk were a framed law degree from Temple University, and a few pictures of people. One was a photograph of a Mummer in full suit and backboard, built to look like a fanned deck of cards behind the wearer; the Joker showed in front. The costume was studded with rhinestones and small, circular mirrors, and festooned with feathers. The man wore full-face makeup. He was a trap drummer, brandishing his sticks and smiling at the camera. Across the bottom someone had written, "Congratulations, Mickey! Quaker City 2014 String Band Champs!" It was difficult to get any sense of the man's build from this photo, but despite the makeup, I recognized his face in another, a promo picture of a club band, five guys in bad tuxes and ruffled shirts. Marcolina appeared to be slight, and shorter than the others.

I checked the desk first, then the file cabinet. I found folders with last names, check stubs from the courts. Marcolina was scuffling – picking up public defender work to supplement his slip and fall clientele. There were motions to suppress evidence, court memoranda, a lot of stuff like that. One of these files concerned a guy with a name I recognized, James Florio. Jimmy had problems stemming from an alleged assault. I noted his contact information and kept looking.

A collection agency was sending Marcolina dunning notices on past due student loans. I got his home address from one of the letters. There was nothing to document any connection to George.

I looked through the lawyer's files for female clients. I found eleven. Four of the women were too old; Marcolina had handled their husband's estates when the guys had kicked. Another was suing the city. She fallen down the stairs at the Municipal Services Building and broken her leg. I eliminated her as a possible based on the injury photos; her ankles were as big around as tree trunks. Pastore wouldn't have looked at her twice, let alone dated her. One more had an unpronounceable name and a child somewhere in China; Marcolina was working the custody case. I doubted that she'd been George's contact, or even a blonde.

None of the remaining five had an address in Center City, but Marcolina may not have updated his records. George had said the woman used to live downtown. I copied the women's names, addresses and phone numbers and left the office. As I crossed the street to my car, I saw a white Mazda Miata parked in front of a driveway in the next block.

*

There were a few guys training in the gym up on the second floor, above the garage on Mifflin Street. One was beating paradiddles on a speed bag in the corner. Jimmy Florio was on the far side of the ring, doing crunches, his arms folded across his chest, his eyes closed. His green tee shirt was soaked black with sweat. He was too old to box any longer. I supposed he enjoyed the workout.

I sat down on a weight bench beside him and said, "Hi, Jim. You know anybody who's got a red Ford van?"

He was startled, stopped exercising and stared for a moment, and said, "No. No, I don't."

"You don't look happy to see me."

"No. Just surprised." He resumed his workout and spoke in rhythm with his repetitions. "What. Do you. Want?"

"What can you tell me about Michael Marcolina?"

"He's. A. Lawyer."

I put my hand on his forehead and held him down. "Enough. Stop and talk like a normal person." His forehead was slippery.

Jimmy was annoyed but sat up and spun to face me. He grabbed a towel hanging from the end of the bar and wiped his face, and wrapped his arms around his shins. His black running shoes looked new but were speckled with white spots. "Painting, Jim?"

"No." He caught his breath and said, "Why you bothering me?"

I took the towel from him and wiped my hand. "I need to find him."

""Who? Oh, yeah, Marcolina. I got no idea where he's at." He unscrewed the cap from a plastic water bottle. "Why would I?"

I put my hand on his wrist. "He's not just a lawyer. He's your lawyer."

He grimaced and said, "I forgot, you're a smart. You wanna take your hand off me, smart guy." I did, and he said, "I don't know him real good. He's just handling some work for me." He took a long drink.

"I saw that. You hit somebody too hard again."

"Hey." Jimmy closed his eyes and shook his head. "I told you I was sorry about that. That guy must've had a condition, or something."

"Yeah. I should have left a note in his pocket, 'not our fault – this guy must have a condition.'"

Jimmy gritted his teeth and said, "I didn't hit him that hard."

"Forget it. I'm just busting your balls. Who told you to go to Marcolina?"

"One of Danny Raco's guys."

I frowned. "Marcolina can't be Raco's lawyer?"

"He's not. Mickey used to work for one of them big law firms in town. Just went out on his own a while ago. You know, he's from the neighborhood – they want to throw some work his way, that's all."

"Sure. Raco and his crew are real benefactors."

"Huh?"

"Forget it. What do you know about Vic Pastore?"

The change of subject threw him for a moment. "I don't know," he said, "he got locked up the other day."

"I know that, too. What's he into?"

"Oh, he's a politician. You know, that kind of stuff."

"What else? Is he hooked up with Raco?"

"I don't know. I mean, yeah, he probably knows him and all, but I don't know if they're like, connected."

"Ok. How would I get to talk to Raco, if I wanted to?"

"I don't know."

"You're a bad liar, Jimmy. I know you still make collections."

"Yeah, I forgot, you're smart." Jimmy frowned while he thought. "You sure you wanna talk to him?"

"No, but if I decide I do, I want to know how."

He took another drink of water, and said, "Look for Jerry, at Men's Finest, up there on the Avenue."

"Men's Finest what?"

"You know, clothes and shoes and stuff."

I pointed at his speckled sneakers. "That where you got your shoes?"

The question flustered him. "I don't remember." He looked down at the shoes and rubbed at the spots, and said, "No, I got them at a chink place, up on Washington Ave." He was still sweating.

"You sure you don't know anybody with a red van?"

"Yeah, I'm sure."

"Take it easy, Jim." I stood up. "Thanks."

He went back to his crunches as I left.

*

I drove up Passyunk Avenue, a skinny, one-way diagonal, well lit, and fronted on either side by stores and restaurants. The new and the old worlds were represented; hipster bars and scooter repair shops sat side-by-side with grocery stores and clothing joints that still sold communion dresses and white shoes. Traffic crawled. The bars and restaurants were busy, and a lot of the other businesses were open late, taking advantage of the crowds.

Joey Giardello's statue occupied a small triangular traffic island described by the cross streets. Its sculptor had depicted the boxer as the hunter he'd been – lean, prowling the ring. A few couples lounged or rested on the benches nearby. I looked at the men. None were Marcolina.

I stopped for the light and studied the people at the intersection. Most were young; most were walking. On the far side, away from the statue were two guys, a little older than most in the crowd, and a little bit rougher. They were tall and wore their hair very short. They were tatted up. Both sported a pair of rings on either hand. Both wore sports shirts, and they were making a point of not looking at anything in particular.

When the light changed, I continued up the Avenue and parked by a hydrant just past Marra's Pizza. A block farther, on the corner at Tasker Street, I saw a men's clothing store, open for business. A rack of sale items stood on the sidewalk in front of the display window. I tried on a green glen plaid sports jacket that was being offered for thirty-five dollars, and did my best to catch my reflection in the plate glass. I checked the sleeve length, held the jacket open and looked at the lining, and glanced back to my reflection.

A salesman came out of the store, watched me and said, "For thirty-five bucks, if you gotta think about it, you should just hang it back on the rack. You ain't gonna buy it." His too-black hair was swept straight back.

I replaced the jacket and said, "You're absolutely right. It's not me."

The man nodded and said, "That's sensible." He pulled out a cigarette and lit up. "What else can I help you with?" He was already looking away, surveying the foot traffic on the Avenue.

"It's Jerry, right?"

He nodded.

"What I'd really like to do is talk to Mr. Raco."

Jerry was good; he didn't show his surprise, just nodded again and said, "You know Danny?"

"Mostly by reputation. I met him once, a few years ago."

"Who are you?"

"My name wouldn't mean anything to him."

He shook his head. "You gotta do better than that."

"I didn't tell him who I was then. He wouldn't have wanted to know." That seemed to register. I added, "You can tell him I'm a friend of George Rafferty."

He said, "I don't think I'll be talking to him tonight."

"That's too bad. He'll want to talk to me."

Jerry thought it over and handed me a card. "Call in an hour or two. I might have something to tell you." He took a last drag, dropped the butt on the pavement and stepped on it, and went back inside the store.

I walked back to the Toyota. There was a ticket under the wiper blade. I dropped it into the gutter and drove away. I was getting impatient. I needed to get a break soon or I'd be out of luck and out of the money.

*

I bought a pay-as-you-go phone in the Asian strip mall at 7th and Washington. A few doors away was a Thai restaurant. I took a seat in the back and ordered the lemongrass soup. The waitress sneered at me. "Ten dollar minimum order to sit at table." I gave her a twenty and told her to go away. A failing air conditioner wheezed away in the transom.

I sat there waiting for the soup and went through the numbers on my list, calling the women who Marcolina had done work for. There was no answer at the first two, only messages to leave a number. On the third I said, "Hello, I'm an associate of your attorney, Michael Marcolina. I'd like to speak with you about recent developments concerning your case—"

"Are you out of your mind? Do you have any idea what time it is?"

I hung up and tried the fourth number. There was no answer, and no answer to the fifth call either. The woman I wanted to speak to might not even be on this list. I was losing patience, and took a few moments to breathe and relax.

There was shouting from the kitchen. The door swung open and closed, and I caught glimpses of the nasty waitress haranguing a Mexican dishwasher – something about spots on the glassware. He'd fashioned himself an outer garment from a large green trashcan liner, in a futile effort to stay dry – he was sweating freely, and he loaded another rack with dirty plates while the waitress yelled at him. He took the chastisement silently.

It was still a surprise to see anyone but an Asian working in an Asian restaurant. As a group, Mexicans were recent arrivals in Philadelphia, and like other paperless immigrants, unlikely to advocate for themselves. Fear of deportation insured their silence. This was an age-old story being played out here: those on the bottom rung of the ladder victimized by those on the next rung up.

I sat back and looked out the front window. Along with the normal street traffic, the two hard guys from Passyunk Avenue walked past.

The waitress brought my soup. I thanked her and asked where the bathroom was. She said something unintelligible and pointed toward the back. I went past the restrooms and through the swinging doors into the kitchen. It was twenty degrees hotter there. The Mexican boy was sweating at the clipper. One of the cooks looked up from a huge wok, frightened. He probably thought that I looked like I.C.E. I winked at him and continued to the screen door in the back.

The waitress pursued me through the kitchen, screaming at me in a combination of Thai and broken English. I pushed through the screen door and out into the alley. She kept yelling. I needed her to shut up. As I spun around and put a finger to my lips, there was a *pop*, and something buzzed past my ear. The shooter tried for me two more times, but I was already diving for a spot behind the dumpster. The rounds skipped off a wall down the alley, leaving small clouds of brick dust in their wake. The waitress screamed and dove back into the kitchen. She and the cooks slammed the steel door shut and shot the bolt.

I didn't know if the hard guys out front heard the silenced weapon, or would move toward or away from the shooting, so I couldn't spend a lot of time here. I stayed low and tried for a look in the shooter's direction. The red van blocked the alley. I ducked back as another shot sounded. The round pinged off the side of the dumpster an inch or so over my head. Paint chips landed on the asphalt.

I checked out the alley behind me. It was bounded by mostly unbroken rows of two-story buildings. Across the alley and down about thirty feet was a run of chain link fence eight feet high. I could be there and up and over in a few seconds but I needed darkness. A light on a pole fifteen feet up the alley lit the area between the fence and me.

The guy with the gun sent a couple rounds through the gap under the dumpster, trying for my ankles. The bullets skipped off the asphalt by my feet. I pulled the twenty-two and fired two shots in the direction of the van, just to make the shooter put his head down, and I shot out the light in the alley. I was up and away as the bulb exploded, before the shooter's eyes could adjust. He sensed movement and let loose with a flurry of shots. One plucked at the sleeve of my shirt as I went over the fence. Another caromed off a metal post and threw up sparks as it squealed away, but I had already dropped to the other side. I heard him bang the van into gear and peel away.

This attack didn't make sense. He had Pastore's safe. He could open it, ditch the van, and be gone. There was no reason to be shooting at me. It was unprofessional.

Unless he thought I knew more about him than I did. As much as I don't like being shot at, his paranoia could help. If he was looking for me, I could still find him and the safe. I came out on the other side of the block and walked back to the Camry.

6

Marcolina's house was on Delhi Street, little more than an alley. I found a spot two blocks away to leave the Camry and walked back to his block, past the market that took up the whole of Ninth Street. A schoolyard backed up to the lawyer's side of the block. His house was in a row of mismatched two and three-story homes. There was a light on upstairs. I knocked and waited. Nothing. I stepped up and looked through the pie-wedge windowpanes in the front door. I could see the stairway, lit from the second floor hall light, and the outline of the living room furniture and past that into the kitchen.

I tried the door. There was no play; the knob was locked along with the deadbolt. The locks were first-class. While I considered the difficulty of getting it all opened, a woman with a little dog came out of a house two doors down. She saw me and said, "Mickey's not home, if you're looking for him." She was short and skinny, maybe in her late sixties.

"Hi." I stepped down to the sidewalk and said, "Who's this guy?" and pointed to the dog, who was straining at the leash to come closer.

She ignored that and said, "Mickey probably won't be around tonight till late. You should probably try him another time, like." She frowned and said, "What happened to your arm?"

I looked; blood trickled from under my shirt's torn sleeve. The shooter had come closer to me than I'd realized. I said, "Must've scratched it on something. Maybe I cut myself shaving." She didn't laugh. I knelt down and ruffed up the fur on the dog's head and neck. "He seems like a very nice boy." The dog licked my hand. "How old is he?"

The woman spoke hesitantly. "He'll be eight this fall." She looked up the street and back.

I petted the dog some more. "That's nice. I had a little dog like this." I gave her a smile. "He's dead now."

To the dog, she said, "Come on, Brutus." The woman pulled at the leash. I held the dog's collar. She said, "What do you think you're doing? I have to go."

"Oh, that's too bad." I picked up the dog and stood. "Do you have any idea where Mickey might have gone tonight? I'd really like to talk to him." I held the dog, my hand under its throat, while I pet him with the other. The woman reached out for the dog. I held him away and said, "Please."

She looked up and down the street for help that wasn't there, and said, "I'm sure I couldn't say." Her voice broke.

"Really? He's practically your next-door neighbor." She reached for the dog again. I smiled but turned away.

Panicked, she grabbed at my shoulder. "Honest, I don't know." She was frightened. Her voice broke again and she said, "Mister, give me my dog. Please." There were tears in her eyes.

"Of course," I said. She wasn't going to be much help. I handed the dog to her. "He's a very nice boy." The woman held the dog close to her and hurried away, and into her house.

I walked back out to Christian Street and hopped the fence to the schoolyard. A seven-foot cinderblock wall separated the playground from Delhi Street's backyards. I counted homes to Marcolina's, reached up and felt along the top of the wall. The masons had set broken glass into the mortar, in an effort to deter thieves. I stripped off my torn sports shirt and my undershirt and wrapped them around my hands, scaled the wall and dropped into a tiny concrete courtyard. There was a patio table and a few chairs, and a rusting Weber grill. A lantern hung from the limb of a junk tree that was growing up out of the corner of the property. Six tiny tomato plants, each just planted and encircled by conical wire cages, were set along the party wall in a swath of unpaved ground, two feet wide, along with some herbs. I could smell the oregano.

The back wall of the home was tan stucco, broken by sliding glass double doors and three windows, one over the kitchen sink and two upstairs.

I pressed my hands to the glass door and pushed up a few times, and heard the lock slip the track. It slid open about an inch and stopped. There was a length of old broomstick handle lying in the frame at the base. I slid the door into it a few times, but the stick was too well seated; I couldn't bounce it out of the channel.

I pulled up one of the tomato cages and shook it free of the plant, and measured it against the width of the door. It was about six inches longer. Not as much as I'd like but it would do. I twisted the heavy wire at the joins between the hoops and one of the verticals. It took some time and my fingers got sore but eventually I'd snapped free a length of the stiff wire about three feet long. I bent a crook into one end and a ninety into the other and slid it through the gap between the frame and the door, and reached for the broom handle with it. In a few tries I managed to hook the length of wood and shift it out of the way. I stepped inside and slid the door closed behind me.

Marcolina's home was small, only about thirty feet deep, a two-story version of a trinity. His laptop was sitting on a small table in the kitchen, but I couldn't get into it without a password. I don't have the skills or the interest for that sort of thing.

There was nothing else downstairs that was of any use to me – no notes in a drawer or stuck to the door of the refrigerator. Upstairs was the same. No home office, nowhere obvious for me to start looking for the woman's name. I was losing patience with the effort.

The bathroom was a surprise for such a small house. It was as big as the larger of the two bedrooms. Along with the tub, toilet and sink, there was a chair in its corner facing the small window, and next to it a little table with an ashtray, a coaster, and a clock radio. Under the table was a wastebasket full of spent lottery tickets. Marcolina's after work ritual must include a shower, a drink and a cigarette while listening for the numbers.

I inspected the wound on my arm in the reflection of the medicine cabinet mirror. The skin around it was bruised, but the cut itself superficial, and had only bled as much as it did because of the effort I'd expended getting over the fence and away from the guy who'd shot at me. I cleaned the wound and dressed it with gauze and tape from the cabinet. Marcolina's shirts were smaller than I needed. I took one – dark gray, short sleeve, slightly larger than the rest – that fit me well enough.

I made to leave by the front door but stopped and moved tight to the inside corner as I saw the two hard guys from Passyunk Avenue through the panes. One stepped up and rattled the knob, and banged on the door while the other peered through the living room window.

I couldn't move from where I was without being seen. If they tried to force the door I'd have to bolt for the rear. I wished I'd left the slider open.

The one at the window said something I couldn't make out, and moved toward the door. I heard a metal on metal sound, and something scratching at the door latch, and I stole a look. He was trying to jimmy the lock with a butterfly knife. I supposed next they'd try to kick the door in.

The old lady with the dog must have decided it was safe to come out again. I heard her say from down the street, "Mickey's getting popular. He isn't home. I told the last fella that, too."

One of them said, "What fella?"

The other told him, "Don't worry about that." To the woman he said, "Where's Marcolina?" He had an accent I couldn't place.

"How should I know? I'm not his mother."

I heard a door open down the street and someone call, "Are you all right, Anna? Is that the same one?"

The guy at the door stepped away and said, "Lady, we asked you question. Where's Marcolina?" He sounded of Eastern Europe.

A door opened across the street. Emboldened, the lady with the dog said, "I don't have to put up with this."

While she had their attention, I moved through the house, went out the back door, and over the wall. I had thought those two were looking for me; now, I wasn't sure.

7

I hesitated at Eighth Street and stole a look toward the Camry before turning the corner. There was somebody sitting on the fender – a guy wearing a hat.

I walked straight through the intersection and continued down Christian, pulled out the burner and dialed the number on the clothes salesman's card. He answered on the second ring, and I said, "This is the sensible guy."

"Right. Mr. Raco will talk to you at his club."

I'd been afraid of that. I said, "Look, I can give you a number where he can reach me if he needs to get to a phone that's safe. I'd prefer to talk to him on the phone."

"He doesn't care what you would prefer, and he never talks on the phone. The club or nothing. What do you want to do?"

I didn't want to go to the man's club for a lot of reasons, but said, "Ok. Where's his club?"

The salesman gave me an address in Queen Village about five blocks from where I stood. This would be tricky. I didn't want a guy like Raco knowing that I existed, but I couldn't keep going around with someone shooting at me, either. If the trouble were coming from his direction, I'd need to convince him that I'd back off.

I walked a few blocks and knelt down by a heavy wire-mesh trashcan that was chained to a pole in front of a darkened sandwich shop. I made as though I was tying a shoelace, but shifted the can on edge and left the target shooter's twenty-two under it.

I walked the rest of the way and knocked on the door of what appeared to be a well-kept, three-story brick row house. Nothing distinguished the building from any of the others on the block, with the exception of an engraved brass plaque, about the size of an index card, mounted on the wall next to the door, which read *Catharine*

Street Social Club. A stocky guy in a sports coat opened the door and stared at me. I said, "I'm here to see Mr. Raco. He expects me."

The guy let me in to a small vestibule, closed the door and motioned for me to turn around, drawing circles in the air with his fat forefinger. I did, and he patted me down efficiently, and said, "Come on, then."

The air-conditioner was running so hard you could've hung meat in there. The doorman walked me through a crowd, past a full bar being tended by two more guys wearing sports coats, to a table in the back where four men sat. The doorman spoke to one of them, "This guy says you're expecting him."

He was an older man, wearing a nice sports jacket. His thin gray hair was plastered across his scalp in a bad comb-over. He looked up and said, "Yeah? I don't know you. What do you want to see me about?"

"Nothing."

"You a smart guy or something? Why you wasting my time?"

"You're wasting mine. I came to see Mr. Raco, not you." I spoke to the man on his right. This guy had snow-white hair, but his mustache and eyebrows were still jet-black. "I only need a few minutes of your time, Mr. Raco."

The dodge with the bald guy must be a regular game that Raco and his crew played. There was only one photograph of Raco that the newspapers or TV stations had, and that was an out of focus shot, taken of him fifteen years before. It caught him in the act of batting away the picture-taker's camera. Danny Raco wasn't a showboat; he protected his privacy. I recognized him from the one time I'd seen him.

He looked younger than he was, but I knew that he had to be in his mid-fifties. He was slender, and had a friendly, relaxed look. He sat there, wearing a thin gold chain and crucifix under his light blue shirt, and looked like any other guy, out with his friends for the night, like he might be a guy who cut hair, or sold real estate. He didn't look like what he was.

His eyes told the truth. They were dark, and hard, and they never stopped moving. He looked at my face, my hands, around me, through me, frisking me with those eyes, and coming back to me again. Raco would make a point of remembering everything.

He stared at me for a few more seconds, and said to the stocky guy, "Thanks, Billy. We'll be all right." The guy nodded and went away. To me, Raco said, "You told Jerry that we've met, but I don't remember you."

"We met at the card game in Longport, a few years ago."

"No," Raco shook his head, "I know everybody at that game."

"I didn't come to play cards."

He got it. He stayed cool but said, "You got some balls, coming here." The other three at the table sat up straighter.

I said, "I didn't know you'd be there. If I'd known that, I'd have never taken the job." Nobody was moving. "I was led to understand that it was all North Jersey guys in that game."

"That didn't stop you, once you saw me."

I shrugged.

"You here to give me back my money?"

"No."

"Then what are you doing?"

"Giving you some information. Maybe doing you a favor."

"Lay it on me."

"George Rafferty's dead."

Raco was quiet for a moment, blessed himself and said, "Ok, you saved me the trouble of looking in the paper. So what? He's been sick a long time, now."

I shook my head. "Somebody killed him." I let that sink in and said, "If you'll talk to me, maybe I can find out who."

"Why should I care about that?"

"Because he did a lot of work for you." Raco thought that over. I added, "He counted you as a friend."

Raco sat there, staring at me and said to the table, "Gentlemen, give us a few minutes." They hesitated. He said, "Go on. This man's just here for conversation, right?" I nodded. The guys at the table got up, staring at me, and moved away. Raco said, "Have a seat."

"Thank you." I took a chair across the table from him.

"You ought to go around with a stocking on your head all the time. It improves your looks." He waited for me to react, and when I didn't, said, "How did George get killed?"

"He got shot. He was doing a job."

"A job with you?"

"Yes."

Raco frowned. "Why didn't you keep that from happening?"

"I was away from him. George got ambushed. Someone was in his shop, waiting."

A waitress came by and asked me, "Can I get you something?"

Raco said, "He isn't staying." He gave her a hundred and said, "Get the fellas a round."

"Sure, Mr. Raco." She left.

He was still frowning. "Would you be this interested if you weren't working with him?"

"No. I liked George, but I don't have any use for revenge. I'm a mechanic. This is about the money."

Raco thought about that and said, "You know I grew up with George?" I nodded. Raco went on, "George never realized his potential. He was always the smartest kid in class, all the way through school. Won scholarships to Villanova and St. Joe's. Did you know that?"

I shook my head.

"This neighborhood is everything to me, but it held George back. His father was a mope. Wanted a son that was good at sports, could fight. That wasn't George. The poor guy was blind as a bat. He wanted to make his old man proud, though. Didn't take any of the scholarships. Joined the Army instead. Paid off a clerk at 401 North Broad to fix the results of his eye exam." Raco shook his head. "He could have been a doctor, gone to work for NASA—"

"Taught at college."

Raco started at the interruption and his expression softened and he said, "George would have been good at anything he wanted to do." He stared at me as though he'd forgotten who I was, and I saw something in his face – a weariness around the eyes – and in that moment I was certain that he regretted his life, that he was tired of all this.

As if he knew he'd given himself away, he frowned and said, "What do you want?"

I said, "I need to know about Vic Pastore. Is he connected?"

"Vic? No, he's nobody in my thing. We help each other out sometimes, but that's all. He sticks to his patch, I stick to mine."

"I would think there'd be more of an overlap."

He shrugged. "Guys like him and guys like me do our best to accommodate each other. It works out better for everybody that way. There's usually enough to go around." He stared at me and said, "Were you and George trying to rip off Vic Pastore?"

I said, "Does he have that kind of reach? To have George killed?"

"No. That's not his thing. He'd do security, maybe a private dick, but nothing heavy. What did you try to take?"

I ignored that and pressed a little. "Pastore might ask someone like you to keep watch on his things for him, while he's away. You or somebody else."

My suggestion wasn't lost on him. He didn't like it, but just said, "He didn't come to me. He's in jail. He's got bigger worries than somebody taking his money. If he's looking for help, it's help staying alive."

"Why's that?"

"Don't act stupid. We both know the government is going to press him. He's been around a long time and knows lots of things, and he could be looking at a long stretch. A lot of guys in politics, and in the life would expect a guy like Pastore to think about trading, and he knows it. His right hand guy, Eddie Reilly – he's already disappeared. You know all this too, so let's not fuck around. What did you guys try to take?"

I pressed a little more. "He's in the Federal Detention Center. Wouldn't a hit there be unlikely? Hard to set up?"

"No. Nobody's really safe anywhere, but it's worse in a place like that. Billy, the guy that let you in here, he's done a lot of time in some really nasty places. He says the worst are the places you go to before anything is settled. Nobody knows who anybody else is. The guy sitting next to you could be an accountant or a psychopath. What did you try to take?"

"Took. A safe."

"From his house?" I nodded. "What did you expect to find when you opened it?"

"There's supposed to be a lot of money in it."

"I doubt that. Who says?"

"One of Pastore's old girlfriends."

"Who is she?"

"I'm trying to find out. Neighborhood girl, originally. She's supposed to have dated him a while. Broke up a few months ago."

"I can't help you. I never knew Pastore well enough to know any of his girls. I know he never stayed with any of them for long. They were always different, but always the same, you know? Same type. If you don't know her, who's your connection?"

"George's connection. A lawyer named Marcolina."

"Oh, Mickey." Raco chuckled. "I got bad news for you, friend. You've been wasting your time."

Either Raco was better than I thought, or his amusement was genuine. "Why am I wasting my time?"

Raco said, "Mickey's a mess. He's a degenerate gambler. Owes money everywhere. Used to owe one of my guys. We straightened him out and cut him off. He got this from a broad? He's terrified of women. It's too bad. He's a good lawyer – really sharp, but he's got bad judgment. I think you should fold that hand."

"Who would he owe money to, now?"

"None of my business."

"There's a couple hard guys running all over the neighborhood looking for him. I assumed they belonged to you, but if they're not yours, he must have trouble with somebody else."

Raco didn't like that, but said, "A man's got a right to collect what he's owed."

"Somebody else is running around here with a gun, a silenced weapon, so I think he's a pro. He's taking shots at people with it."

"You mean he's taking shots at you?"

I pushed a little harder. "I would think that another boss might give you a head's up about something like that. Before coming in to your neighborhood to do business."

Raco snapped. "Do you think you're telling me something I don't know? Or are you just trying to rub my nose in shit?"

"Sorry. None of my business, then."

Raco didn't say anything to that. I said, "If I find Marcolina, I can find the woman, and then maybe whoever did George."

"And took Pastore's safe."

"My safe."

Raco smiled at that. "Where have you looked for Mickey so far?"

"His office, his house."

"Mickey plays in a band most weekends. If he's not playing, then he went somewhere to lose money. But again, I think you're chasing a bad pony."

"What makes you say that?"

"Because Pastore isn't stupid. He wouldn't have left cash in that house. He'd have hid it better."

"Where?"

"Where do you think? A safety deposit box, or offshore, in a blind account." He thought for a moment and said, "Maybe nowhere. I've heard that lately he has money worries."

"Why's that? He's supposed to be loaded."

"Yeah, but it's all tied up. He owns real estate all over the place, houses and what not. I heard lately he sold a place just to make his monthly note. Sold it at a loss. I heard he's been moving stuff around."

"What stuff?"

"Stuff. Things – property. His boat. It's still his, but I hear he put it in somebody else's name."

"What happened to him?"

"What happens to anybody? You have a bad month. You lose money on the wrong deal. Sometimes that's all it takes. Your time would be better spent talking to Eddie Reilly, if you can find him." Raco looked annoyed. "That's all you got?"

I nodded.

"That's pretty thin. What else you gonna do for me?"

"I've done a lot for you already."

"How about the name of the guy that helped you in Longport?"

"Wouldn't do you any good. He's dead."

"Just like George." When I didn't react, he said, "A name might do me a lot of good."

Raco was too real to make direct threats, but I got it. I changed the subject. "You know anybody who drives a red Ford van? Jersey tags?"

"Who doesn't?" The question didn't seem to faze him. "There must be a million of those trucks on the road."

I stood up. "Thanks."

"You still gonna try and run this down?"

"Maybe." I could see that it was time to kiss the ring, so I said, " As long as you have no objections, of course."

Raco ignored that and said, "If you do get a hold of that can, I want whatever else you find in it, any paperwork, any tapes, discs, whatever."

"What for?"

"You don't worry about what for. You just get it to me. This here," he waved his hand back and forth between us, "this is just a time-out. You want to get square with me, you do what I want."

I nodded and left.

8

I recovered the pistol and walked back to the Camry. The man with the hat was still hanging around, sitting on the fender. There wouldn't be any point in trying to come behind him, so I walked up and said, "Get off my car."

The man chuckled and stood up. "You've been a busy guy."

I made to unlock the door. "I'm still busy."

The man said, "Uh-uh." His wallet was in his hand. He held it open to show a seven-pointed badge and said, "Sheriff's. Don't go anywhere yet." He made a point of holding his fingers over the name on his ID card. "We have things to talk about." He folded the wallet and put it in his front pocket. "Relax. I can help you." I waited. Finally, he smiled again and said, "Sorry. It's been a long day for me too." He took off his hat and scratched his shaved head. "You're too careful to leave prints. I ran your car. That gave me a name that I'm sure isn't really yours." He put his hat back on. "It's the name of someone who lives at an address that doesn't exist anymore. But, it's a name – you may have used it somewhere else. And, I got some really good pictures of you going in and out of Pastore's place." He waited for a few seconds and said, "Still nothing to say? That's all right. I know – a fake name, a few pictures. It isn't a lot. But it's a place to start. That's the thing about police work: a place to start is half the game. Once you have that, well, you're a smart guy, I don't have to explain it to you."

"You're not police."

He chuckled again. "I work warrants. I'm close enough."

If he did have them, my prints wouldn't connect to anyone or anything, but I still didn't want this guy to get them. The man was right; prints, or that name and a picture could be enough to wreck what I had built up here, or at least make things less comfortable. I didn't want to have to start over. "What do you want?"

"I want what's inside that safe you took. Some of it, anyway. Don't worry, I'm not an animal. We can come to a fair agreement."

"Help yourself. I don't have squat."

"You're not using your imagination. You must have something, some idea, all the running around you've been doing. Give me a name, or an address, or a phone number and we're in business."

We'd never be in business. I'd dump him as soon as I could. He would try to do the same thing, but would probably know that he'd have to kill me to do it.

I did want to see where this would go. I said, "I have the phone number of a guy who helped finger the job. I've never met him, but he might know something useful."

"Give me the number." I took Marcolina's card from my pocket. The deputy reached for it, but I held it away and read the number to him. He chuckled and took out his phone. "This'll take a few minutes," he said, as he punched numbers.

He was going to track the phone by GPS. I said, "What if this guy doesn't have a smart phone?"

He turned his back on me and spoke under his breath. He was an idiot. I thought about dropping him there in the street, but waited. I wanted to see what he could do. After about fifteen seconds, he turned and said, "They'll call me back in a minute or two. To answer your question, it doesn't matter what kind of phone he's got, or even if it's turned on. We can find it." He held up his phone and said, "I love The Patriot Act." The phone rang; he answered, and said, "Ok. Thank you and have a good night."

To me he said, "Saddle up." He put the phone in his inside jacket pocket. "I know where he is."

"Where's that?"

He said, "Why don't you just drive and leave the navigating to me?" We got into the car. "Go north on Fifth Street." He got settled in and buckled his seatbelt. I drove around the corner and saw the Miata parked halfway up the block. He rolled down the window and leaned his arm on the doorframe.

I was working out a way to lose this guy once I knew where we were going. "Put your window back up. I'll turn on the AC."

"What are you talking about? It's nice out."

"Nobody's making you ride in this car."

He chuckled and rolled it up.

I took the left on Fifth and said, "I'm pretty low on gas. How far are we going?"

"Not far." He leaned over to look at the gauge. It read a little under half a tank. "You'll be all right." He settled back in.

The row houses gave way to townhouses and big singles as we came into Old City. Past Independence Mall, he said, "Take the tunnel under the bridge."

I wanted to know more about this guy. I said, "If you've been watching things, why didn't you follow George to his shop?"

"I knew where he was going and what he would be doing."

"He could have opened it up and been gone."

"It would take a while for him to open up that box. If you guys were safecrackers you'd have done it on-scene and saved yourselves the heavy lifting. I had time. I wanted to see where you were going. You're the wild card."

He was either lying or stupid. The only thing to do in his position would be to follow the money. I said, "I checked that intersection really well. I'd have seen you if you were in a car anywhere near there."

He was quiet for a few moments, thinking about how much to give me, and finally said, "I was in an apartment, up the street from Pastore's. My car was out front."

He was lying. He hadn't expected George to take off, he'd been waiting for me to come out and ride along, which meant he was out of his element – didn't understand the way professionals worked. It was all about limiting exposure. George wasn't doing anything that anyone could charge him with until the safe was in his possession. That was why he left as soon as he had it in the trunk. I couldn't be charged with anything more than breaking and entering until the safe went out the window, which was why I'd left empty-handed. If either of us had gotten caught, neither would jeopardize the other. I wouldn't sell out George; I had a reputation, and giving up a partner would ruin it. George knew it wouldn't be worth his while to talk about me.

I said, "Where to?"

"Take a right at Spring Garden."

I guessed at where we were headed, and knew how I'd get rid of this guy. I liked the Camry; it was easy on gas and handled well, but it was burned. As I expected, he had me turn left onto Delaware Avenue. The docks and warehouses were gone, but traffic was still thick on the big road, the clubs and strip joints were busy.

We were coming up to The Sugarhouse Casino. The deputy said, "Ok, this is where we want to go. I think the parking garage is just up here." He pointed past the casino.

Nothing hurts as badly as when you don't see it coming. I braced myself and jerked the wheel hard to the left into on-coming traffic. A mini-van slammed into the passenger door. The deputy's head shattered the passenger window; he was rocked, dazed. My shoulder hurt, but I undid his seat belt, and slammed his head into the dashboard. I took his service pistol from his holster and slid the target-shooter's twenty-two in its place. He was moaning and grabbed at my hand. I bounced his head off the dashboard again, and he was still.

I lifted my shirttail to slide the bigger gun into my waistband. I took his wallet, keys and cuffs. There was an envelope in his inside jacket pocket, along with his phone. I took them both, as well. After giving the Camry's interior a quick wipe, I got out of the car, rotating my shoulder. I was shaken up, but okay.

Steam geysered from the mini-van's grill; I could hear the ticking of the contracting metal parts over the ringing of my ears. Its driver-side windshield was starred – cracked, and bulged outward in an irregular, round shape – that was probably from the air bag; the driver was still in his seat, but moving.

A car stopped, and another slowed, each driver looking over the damage. They displayed the typical amount of shock and confusion at any accident scene. Another car slowed. It was time to go. As I trotted away, somebody called out, "What are you doing?"

I kept moving and flagged down a cab two blocks from the wreck.

9

I had the driver head toward Center City. While I rode, I checked out the deputy's things. The pistol was a Glock 19, with a ten round magazine. His iPhone held a lot of pictures. Some of them were of George and me. He hadn't sent them anywhere, as far as I could tell. Anyway, the pictures of me were too poor to be definitive.

I paged through his contacts listing. Most were first names. They didn't provide me any help. I looked at his Favorites. There were four, all women: Lucy, Anna, Brenda and Margaret. None matched the names of any of Marcolina's clients. It was frustrating; I didn't know what I was looking for.

No one he was connected with would know that anything had happened to him, at least for a while. I considered holding onto his phone, in the hope that someone involved with him would call, and that I might be able to impersonate him and glean some information that would prove helpful, but realized how stupid that sounded as I thought about it. Plus, he'd just shown me how easily law enforcement could locate a cell phone.

I dropped his phone to the floor of the cab and hammered it with the butt of the pistol four or five times. The cabbie said, "What the fuck are you doing?"

"Shut up." I opened the window and dropped the phone on the roadway, while keeping my eyes on the cabbie's in the rear-view mirror. The man looked back and forth between the road and me but stayed quiet.

I went through the deputy's wallet. He had a little less than three hundred dollars in cash, all in twenties. His name was Joe Dougherty. His driver's license listed an address on Fitzwater Street, near 4th. Besides his Sheriff's ID, he had platinum Visa and Master cards, and registration cards for the 2012 Mazda Miata that I had seen, and a 1994 Jaguar. It all seemed like a lot for a guy who was supposedly living on sergeant's pay. His cards and ID should all be good for a few hours; Dougherty would be out for a while, and not very communicative for a while after that. I slipped the Visa credit card out of his wallet and into my hip pocket.

I had choices. I needed to see if Tom knew why things had fallen apart tonight. Tom probably wouldn't know much; he wouldn't have asked George a lot of questions, but he still might be able to help me. I also needed to grab Marcolina. Both could keep. Tom would be working and Marcolina would be at the casino until his money ran out. The smart thing to do now was to let myself into Dougherty's place with his keys. He was crooked and stupid. He'd have cash at home. I read his address to the cabbie and sat back.

I opened the envelope. Inside was a court order, a writ for Pastore's release from federal detention, signed by The Honorable D. M. D'Allesandro. It was post-dated for the next day. I stuffed it back in the envelope and into my hip pocket.

The hack slowed as we turned onto Dougherty's block, but I saw the red van on the far corner, parked by a hydrant and said, "Keep going, keep going." Along with the driver, there was someone in the passenger seat now, too; I could see his silhouette through the van's back window. As we rolled past I looked, but couldn't make out much about him, or the driver.

I considered going back and taking them, but gave up on the idea. The approach would be difficult; they would certainly be vigilant. If they saw me before I could get to them, it would be two on one, and the driver had already demonstrated his skills with a handgun. I had to assume the passenger would be armed as well. I'm never interested in a fair fight, let alone going in outnumbered. Also, this was a nice, quiet neighborhood; gunfire here would be unusual. It's reporting, and the resulting police response would both be swift. If I were able to take them both, I'd have to commandeer the van, and would be driving the big, red vehicle the police would be looking for – with two bodies inside it. Most importantly, I couldn't know if the safe was still in the van. Professionals wouldn't be driving around the city with obviously stolen property in their possession. I'd be back to square one – looking for my safe.

What was interesting was that they knew Dougherty — knew him well enough to know where he lived. Assuming that they were connected, why were they waiting outside his house?

I said to the cabbie, "Take me to The Idle Hour." I sat back and rode the rest of the way to the bar in silence, disgusted, and paid the fare with one of Dougherty's twenties.

Inside, there were seven or eight patrons nursing drinks. Some of them were staring at a television mounted in the corner. The Phillies were down two runs in the second. I took a seat at the bar as far away from any of the other patrons as I could. Tom was busy taking bottles of beer out of the cooler and pushing them into the ice chest next to the sinks as he spoke into a phone cradled between his head and shoulder. The phone cord tethered him to the counter, restricting his movements; he frowned as he listened and said, "Then you're gonna have to go back down there in the morning and look around some more. I told you last night I wasn't sure." Tom noticed me and said, "Look, call me back when you're done, I got a lot going on. I'll talk to you later." He hung up the phone, slid the cooler door closed, and walked toward me while he dried his hands on a towel. All of his movements were deliberate and unhurried. He didn't smile, but said, "How you doing?" and laid a coaster on the bar in front of me.

I put up another of Dougherty's twenties. "Let me have a club soda, and get yourself a drink."

He poured the soda, and took a beer from the ice. He felt it and said, "Cooler crapped out on me, earlier. I got a call in to a guy but he hasn't gotten back to me yet." He twisted off the cap. "Timing couldn't be worse. First hot week of the year." He took a sip, and said, "You must need something."

I nodded. "Mostly information. What do you know about Vic Pastore?"

"Not a lot." He pitched the bottle cap into a trashcan. "He doesn't come in here, much.

I wasn't in the mood for Tom's sarcasm. "George Rafferty's dead. Somebody shot him."

Tom looked like he'd been punched in the gut. He opened his mouth to speak but didn't.

I added, "He said you told him to call me."

"Hey, whoa." He put a hand up. "He was looking for help and I knew you were available. He didn't tell me anything about the job." He brushed back his silvery hair with his fingers.

I watched him and said, "It was a guy in a red van. Sound like anyone you know?"

Tom didn't react, he just said, "No." He took a bottle down from the back shelf, poured himself two fingers and drank it off, and refilled his glass. He added, "George shouldn't have been anywhere near any rough stuff."

I ignored that and said, "I have a line on the guy who fingered this, a guy named Marcolina." Tom shook his head. I continued, "If you can give me anything about Pastore, it would help."

Tom spoke distractedly, "I really don't know any more than you could get from the papers. He made his load in real estate. Well, his old man did. Vic just built on it." He thought some more and said, "No, not really." He seemed to remember the bottle in his hand, and said, "Have one?"

"No thanks. Do you know anybody in the Sheriff's?"

He glanced to his right and said, "Gimme a minute," and got drinks for two guys at the far end of the bar. I looked up at the Phillies game, and then at a framed citation from the Fraternal Order of Police hung next to the television.

Tom came back. He said, "I broke George in. Did you know that?"

I hadn't thought that Tom was that old, but just said, "No. I didn't."

"Poor George was not cut out for patrol. He tried – he wasn't a coward – but it was never quite enough, you know? Lousy shot, too. I'm glad we never got into anything heavy. He was fun to work with, though. Smart guy."

"How'd he get into Major Crimes, then? Connections?"

"Uh-uh." Despite himself, Tom chuckled silently. "George was installing pirate HBO antennas. Had a nice little sideline going, until he got caught. Big uproar. Lot of people wanted him fired. This one Chief Inspector, Fitzpatrick, he tells the Commissioner, 'leave it to me, I'll straighten George out.' What he did, he had George install antennas at his house, each of his daughters, a bunch of his friend's places. The gift that keeps on giving. Fitzy got George off the street, though."

Tom seemed lost in thought for a moment. The bar's phone rang. He put up a finger and answered. "Yeah, hi, Benny. Can you come out tonight?" He waited, and said, "That's all right. I'll be here by eleven. I can be here earlier, if it helps, but I'd rather not fight bridge traffic if I don't have to. No? Okay. Look, if you can't fix it, do you have anything that'll fit in that space? All right, I'll see you tomorrow." He ended the call and stared at the cooler, thinking about his tepid beer.

I brought him back around. "I need a couple other things."

"Oh, yeah?"

"Yeah, you know anybody in the Sheriff's?"

"Sorry. I don't know any of those guys, there. You'd just see them in the courthouse, say hello, that's about it."

"Don't they have guys on the street, too?"

"Some, serving papers, subpoenas. Real estate stuff, mostly – foreclosures and things like that – but most of their guys do prisoner transport."

"Don't they have guys working warrants?"

"Yeah, that too, but I don't think there's many doing that. That's maybe like twenty, thirty guys. Like I said, I don't know a lot about them. Why?"

"Just curious." Tom looked annoyed. I said, "I might need a car. Something that can move."

"Why not go to Lon?"

"I think he's having trouble."

Tom nodded and said, "You got money on you?"

"Some. I can get more if I need it."

He wrote a phone number on a bar napkin. "Ask for Flipper. He's a smoke, but he's okay. You can tell him I sent you." He handed me the napkin and began to move away.

I said, "Hey." Tom turned back toward me. "I'm looking at a long night. You got anything to help with that? Anything that won't whack me out?"

"I can give you some Ritalin. Generics. Eight for fifty."

"Ok." I slid two twenties and a ten onto the bar. He took the money and pushed through the swinging doors into the kitchen.

Bells sounded in the corner. I glanced over. A barfly was feeding money into the poker machine. On the wall above that was a small wood and brass plaque from the police marine unit, next to a flickering Guinness promotional neon.

Tom left a towel on the bar in front of me, and walked back to his failing cooler. I finished my drink and reached under the towel. A pill bottle was there. I knew better than to rattle it.

10

I made a call on my way to the casino. "Hey, it's me. Open up that spot behind the baseboard and take out five thousand. I'll be by for it in a while." If I was going to need a car, I'd need to pay cash. I had Dougherty's keys, but his Miata was too flashy for me to use.

Down the street from The Sugarhouse, the cars had been towed away and the debris pushed to the curb. I walked up the stairs and went inside the casino. It looked bright and loud, and gaudy, but it was essentially a low-ceilinged catering hall, full of old people pissing away their pension checks. One lady sat in front of a slot machine with a bucket of nickels on her lap, patiently feeding them into the machine, one by one. Her eyes looked glazed over. She sipped from a drink in a plastic cup, and she almost looked as though she'd be pissed off if she won – it would break her concentration.

I spotted Marcolina at one of the blackjack tables – recognized him from the pictures in his office. He was sitting hunched over, fiddling with his chips as the cards came to the players. He had a six showing and took a hit; the dealer shot him a nine, and Marcolina sat back in his chair, looking disgusted. He flipped his hold card, an eight. The dealer raked in his cards and chips. Marcolina had a handful of chips left, which he stacked and restacked, compulsively. Tattooed onto the back of his right hand, on the web between his thumb and forefinger, was a faded treble clef.

I tapped him on the shoulder and said, "You need to come with me."

Marcolina looked up, annoyed. "Who are you?"

"Don't worry about it." I could tell then that he recognized my voice and realized who I was. "Just get up and come with me."

His face went from annoyed to worried and then blank. "I'm in the middle of a game here." He faced the table. I spun him around in his seat. He said, "What are you doing?" A fat blond woman sitting next to him watched us. He took a good look at me and said, "Hey, that's my shirt."

The dealer said, "Is everything all right, sir?" He looked past us for help.

I took out Dougherty's wallet and flashed his badge. "It is as long as this man comes with me." I put my hand on Marcolina's arm.

The dealer said, "Of course." He began dealing a hand to the others.

I said to Marcolina, "Pick up your chips. You can cash out later."

He put them in the pocket of his sports coat. "I hope this won't take too long."

I didn't say anything, just led him outside and into the parking lot. "Where's your car?"

"Over this way. What are you —"

"Why weren't you where you said you'd be?"

"Hey, there were a couple of monsters on the Avenue. I couldn't wait around and I couldn't get in touch with you."

"I called. You didn't answer."

"My battery died."

I smacked him on the side of his head. "Ow!" He staggered a step and recovered. "What was that for?"

I grabbed his arm and walked us in the direction of the car. "Who shot George?"

"What? Somebody shot George? How is he?"

I believed him. Marcolina was really shocked. I said, "Dead. And the thing we took is gone."

"Fuck." He kept his hand on the side of his head. "Fuck. That wasn't supposed to happen."

I crowded him. "What *was* supposed to happen?"

"No, hey, look, I mean, it was supposed to be the way Brenda said – easy – no problems." He looked around the parking lot. "Fuck." He rubbed his eyes with the heels of his hands. "I need that money." He looked up at me and said, "Look, I'm not interested in this anymore. I'm no hard guy. I just want to go home and forget all about this."

"It's too late for that. Who's the guy in the red van?"

"Who? What van?"

"Red Ford Econoline," Marcolina was no card player. He didn't know what I was talking about, but I kept going, "Jersey plates. Who is he?"

"No, really, I have no idea. What did he do?"

I wanted to keep him off-balance. "What's Brenda's last name and where is she now?"

"Huh? Oh, I can't tell you that."

"Sure, you can."

"No. She was really clear, she didn't want to deal with anybody but me."

"Like I said, it's too late for all that." He was still shaking his head no. I said, "I'm not going to spend a lot of time on nonsense."

"All right. Brenda Michaels. I know her from the neighborhood."

"Where is she right now?"

"I don't know."

I must have looked annoyed. He said, "Honest to god, I don't know." He held his hands out. "Why would I need to know where she is? Her part is done, right?"

I thought about it. "How were you going to settle up with her?"

"She was gonna call me tomorrow. We'd figure it out from there."

"Call her now."

"I already tried once, tonight. Her phone is off."

"Why'd you try her tonight?"

"You know – to see if she wanted to get together, maybe."

"Where does she live?"

"On Pine Street. Near Rittenhouse Square."

"All right." We were in the far corner of the lot. "Which is your car?" He pointed to a black Saab. I said, "This looks a little bit too extravagant for someone in your circumstances."

"To tell you the truth, it is. I got it special, through a friend of mine that usually cuts them up for parts. You know. The papers look real, but they're actually from a car that was totaled out and went to the scrap yard."

I had the picture now. Marcolina was a wanna-be; he was desperate to be a wise guy.

He said, "What about the guy in the van? Who is he?"

"He has our things." We got into his car. "Take us to Penn's Landing."

Marcolina frowned. "What are we gonna do there?"

"Look for a boat."

*

I didn't know for certain that Pastore's boat would be in the marina at Penn's Landing, but it seemed likely, given its location and Pastore's penchant to be ostentatious. We pulled past the marina into the parking garage. Marcolina grabbed the ticket and drove until he found a spot on the second level, but I told him to keep going, all the way to the top. He pulled into a space up on the roof, under the stars, and made to get out. I said, "No. You stay here." I held out my hand. "Keys."

He hesitated, handed the set to me and said, "Wait, why should I be up here? I could help you –"

I snapped one of the cuffs around his right wrist. He said, "Aw, come on, man." I yanked his arm through the steering wheel, pulling him down, reached under the dash and snapped the other cuff around the brake pedal shaft, leaving his face and chest crushed up against the wheel. "Jesus, man. Come on. This is demeaning."

"I won't be long." I held up his business card. "Don't even think about yelling for help or trying to skip out on me. I've already been inside your house and your office."

"What? Why were you in my – " It was all coming too fast for him. He gave up and said, "No, no, I'm not going anywhere. Obviously." I walked away. He called out, "Hey, don't take too long. I gotta pee."

I took the elevator down and walked toward the marina entrance. There was a guard in a booth at the foot of the walkway. I walked the length of the marina's frontage but couldn't find another way inside. I went half way back to the entrance and loitered there until a group of three couples came out of the parking garage. I caught up and fell in behind them. The guard smiled and waved them through, and me along with them. A dozen steps inside, I broke away and walked down one of the docks handling the larger boats.

The place was lit up like a stadium at night. The rest of the city was shrouded. Across the river, The Camden Aquarium stood out from most of the properties along the waterfront. Downriver from there, arc lights on poles lit the Camden County Detention Center.

Most of the berths were full, the boats ranging in size from little one-mast fifteen footers to something just this side of the Queen Mary. There were parties on some of them, lots of music and drinking. A woman called out to me from one; I couldn't make out what she said but I smiled and waved as I went by. I walked up and down the docks looking for "Mover 'n Shaker."

Few people pay any attention to someone who moves deliberately. I found the boat nestled between two like it, and stepped up, over the gap and the rail, and onboard. Pastore's boat was a Viking Salon Sportfisher. Its enormous fly bridge soared over the waterline. I opened the door to the staterooms easily enough, raking the pins twice. People with boats like this counted on location and personnel to keep them secure, not locks. I put my tools away and went inside.

Below deck, the boat was spotless. It smelled of bleach. There were two staterooms – each with a head and a shower – and a galley. This boat would have been able to comfortably accommodate half a dozen people, and a lot more if they weren't picky, but for one thing – there was nothing on board, no provisions of any kind, no food, no bedding, no spare clothes, no fishing equipment – nothing. In a cabinet by the wheel was a book, a log. I paged through it. There were entries that went back a few years – cursory information, sketched out in a sort of shorthand – what looked like dates, times, fuel purchases. Here and there were occasional remarks in longhand, *Blues running today – took limit in half an hour* or, *Note: tell Reilly not to invite D'Allesandro again.* The latest entry was dated last year, in late November.

I finished searching the vessel and stepped back over the rail onto the dock. As I walked back toward the gate, a guy sitting on the fantail of a small sailboat, said, "Hi. Nice night," he looked up and added, "if it doesn't rain." His boat was a Pearson. It looked like an older model, but well kept up. The guy was alone, sipping from a bottle of Ballantine Ale. He'd been looking off in the direction of Camden. He was probably in his fifties, but still had most of his hair, most of it still dark, and he looked at the world through thick lens, horned rim glasses that made his eyes look smaller than they were. He pointed out on the river and said, "Those guys sure have been busy tonight. Those, and the Coast Guard guys."

I looked; a city fireboat, the "Bernard Samuel," cruised upriver, past the marina. A crewmember on deck raked the water ahead of them with a light

The guy continued, "You taking Pastore's boat out?"

"Doesn't look like it. I was supposed to meet some guys here, but I don't think they're going to show. You haven't seen anybody on his boat tonight, have you?"

"Who are you?"

"A friend of Vic's."

The guy chuckled and said, "I didn't know Vic had any friends any more. Except for the friends that use his boat. These last few months, they've used it a lot." He slurred a little on the words "friends" and "use."

"Isn't that odd? Going out in the winter?"

He considered this and said, "Yeah, for most people. Yeah. Some guys go out for stripers, out past the bay, but that's not my idea of fun."

"But you're here to see them go out. You must like it."

"I just like to sit out here at night, sometimes, you know? It's pretty, the lights and all." He chuckled, apologetically. "I don't take it out in the cold weather." I nodded. He laughed some more and said, "How do you know Vic?"

"From around."

"Right. Vic's friend. From around." He took a swallow and said, "You don't look like the kind of guy that would be Vic's friend."

"No?"

He shook his head.

I said, "What do Vic's friends look like?"

"Like Vic." He seemed to think that was funny, and laughed at his own joke. "Not the friends he lends his boat to, though. Not lately. They don't look like Vic, either." He stared at me and said, "They look more like you."

"Who are they?"

The man ignored that and said, "I went to The Prep with Vic. Scholarship. He pretends not to remember who I am, but he does."

I was beginning to figure this guy for a dead end – a bitter, lonely drunk, sitting on his little boat on a Friday night, but I humored him. "Why's that?"

The man took a swallow and stared across the river. Then he said, "Vic got all his growth early. In tenth grade he was as tall as he is now, almost six foot, and probably went as much as one-ninety. Sad thing was, his voice still hadn't changed." He chuckled to himself. "Here's this big asshole with this squeaky little kid's voice. Comical." He stopped smiling and continued, "He liked to push the little guys around, him and his buddy, Reilly. Thought it was funny. One day in the lunchroom, I'm talking to this kid, this friend of mine, and Vic walks by and sticks his finger in the kid's mashed potatoes, and laughs. Reilly, too, they're laughing their asses off. I told them to knock it off. Vic says, 'What are you gonna do about it?'" The guy let me mull that over while he took a sip of his beer, and said, "I beat the shit out of him. Blacked both his eyes. He was crying like a little girl. Reilly ran away, to tell the priests." He took another sip and smiled at the memory.

"Of course, his old man got involved. The priests loved Vic's old man. He tried to get me expelled. I ended up with two-week's suspension, and detention for the rest of the semester. I lost my scholarship the next year, which was as good as kicking me out. I finished up at Central, but it was worth it." He emptied the bottle and dropped it into a plastic five-gallon bucket, opened his cooler and took out another beer. He looked at me and said, "Have one?"

"No thanks."

He opened the bottle with a church key that was strung to the cooler handle with twine, and chuckled. "Now, any time Vic goes by, I wave to him. He pretends not to see me, but he does." He took another swallow and said, "The guys using his boat aren't as friendly as you are. Who did you say you were?"

"I'm a guy who wants to know where that boat's been going."

"Why's that?"

"Because I'd like to see Vic stay right where he is for a while."

He thought about that for a few moments. "The Coast Guard recommends you share your travel plans with the harbormaster. You should. It's good to have somebody, knows where you are. But I wouldn't be surprised if those guys skip that."

"That doesn't help me."

He stared at me as though he'd lost his train of thought, but said, "They always head south, toward the bay. Never gone for more than a few hours. They take fishing gear with them, but never catch anything." He took a sip of beer and looked back toward Camden. "A funny thing – the one guy always comes back by himself."

"That is funny. Where do you think the other guy gets off?"

"Somewhere else." He chuckled. "That's all I can tell you about that. Hope it helps."

"Do you know what they drive?"

"Sorry. Why would I?"

11

I thanked the guy and hustled back to the garage, undid the cuffs and let Marcolina pee behind the car, and told him to get in the passenger seat. I pulled out of the garage, and drove us toward the woman's house. I said, "How do you know George?"

"Through music, mostly. We've both played in each other's bands, you know, filling in when the regular guys couldn't make it."

"And one thing leads to another?"

"Yeah, you know how it is. You talk with a guy, and you find out what he does, and yeah, one thing leads to another."

"How long have you known him?"

"Oh, I don't know. A while."

"That's a little strange, isn't it? George was a good bit older than you."

"Yeah, but that doesn't matter so much with music. George kept up with new tunes. He wasn't great, but he could handle the changes and play in time. And man, he was the best if something went wrong with the equipment. Really good at fixing stuff in a pinch."

"Yeah. I suppose he would be."

"That's how he got into electronics in the first place – fixing amps and stuff. Still does that from time to time."

"You represent Jimmy Florio."

"Jimmy," he chuckled, "yeah. He had some trouble."

"Can you get him off?"

"I will if there's a woman on the jury. He's a good-looking guy."

We rode for a minute and I said, "Who takes your action?"

"Well, you know, different guys. I spread it around."

"No. Raco told me he cut you off. He says you're bad pay. Word gets around that you're a deadbeat and most pros don't want to bother with you. So answer my question. Who takes your bets now?"

He stalled for a moment and said, "This guy I met at the C.J.C. Anton. Eric Anton. Foreign guy, Ukrainian or something."

"Or something?"

"Hey, sometimes it's best not to ask those guys too many questions, you know? He's from somewhere in Eastern Europe."

"Where do you go to pay him off when you lose?"

"Funny. You're a funny guy. I settle up with him at La Colombe, at Rittenhouse Square. A lot of those foreign guys like to hang out at places like that – coffee bars. It's a scene."

We slowed going past the FOP. There was no parking available anywhere near the entrance. Marcolina said, "You want to go here?"

"Yeah. I need to find out about a few things."

I went around the block and parked. The ass end of Marcolina's car broached the mouth of a driveway. He started to protest, but lost the thread as I grabbed his wrist. As I pulled out the cuffs, he said, "Aw, come on, man. Not again."

"I have to do something with you. I can't let you run loose."

He tugged away from the cuffs. "No, look, that's not necessary. I'm invested in this effort. I have a stake."

"I can't leave you here."

"I'll come in with you. I can help. I used to work for the firm that represents these guys. Just tell me what you want to do."

I mulled it over while I stared at him. He was a gambler; his need for money would probably outweigh any idea of throwing me under the bus in order to extricate himself from the situation. He also looked curious, like he wanted to see where this would go. He could cause me a lot of trouble if he wanted, but he had to know that it would come back on him.

As if he read my mind, he said, "I'm not stupid enough to try anything."

"Ok." I let go of his wrist and put the cuffs away. "We're going inside to find someone from the Sheriff's."

"Who?"

"Anybody who can tell us about a Deputy I met an hour ago. Come on."

He flipped down the visor and checked himself in the vanity mirror, brushing his hair with his fingers and straightening his tie. "Ok." He got out of the car, worried again about my park job, and walked with me to the hall.

I showed the man at the door Dougherty's badge and said, "This guy's with me." The guy ignored me and said, "Mister Marcolina, how you doing?"

"I'm good, Franny. What's going on?"

"Not a great night. We just got word a little while ago – a retired cop got killed, over there in Franklintown."

Marcolina said, "Yeah, we heard that. George Rafferty. Horrible. I know George from the neighborhood. Played in bands with him." I prodded him and he continued, "You hear anything more about that?"

"No, not really. He was shot. Looked like maybe he was robbed."

Marcolina moved to let a couple past us and said, "How's your brother?"

"He's an asshole." To the couple, the doorman said, "Sorry. Youse enjoy yourselves." They went inside and he looked back to Marcolina and said, "I haven't seen him. If he hasn't called you, I guess he's okay. What's going on? I never seen you here before."

"Oh, yeah, I've been here once or twice. We're looking for some help with a thing."

"Anything I can do?"

"I don't think so, Fran. I just need to look around."

"Ok. You take care." He looked past us and spoke to a group of women who'd come to the door. "Hello, ladies, great to see youse."

We went inside. It was loud. The bar was three-deep. The dance floor was crowded; about fifty people, mostly women, were line dancing. Marcolina nodded toward them "Some things never go out of style."

Most of the patrons were in civilian clothes, but there were a few uniforms. I propelled Marcolina toward the bar; he was trying to scope out the women on the floor. Marcolina knew the bartender, too, and said, "I'll have –"

I broke in, "Two club sodas."

Marcolina grimaced and said, "Yeah, two sodas, please." He pulled a ten out of his wallet. The bartender poured the drinks and set them in front of us. He waved away the money. Marcolina said, "Thanks," and handed me a soda.

I said, "You're a popular guy."

"The thing about cops is, when they make a mistake, they've usually broken some laws, too. Then they need help." He shrugged. "What can I say? I'm a good lawyer." He looked around the room and said to me, "I've only been in this place a few times. I'd come more, but I never liked the idea of being the only guy in a bar who wasn't carrying a gun, you know?" While he spoke he scanned the crowd. He caught the eye of a red haired woman and waved to her.

I tapped his shoulder. "We aren't here for fun."

"Right, right. We want somebody from the Sheriff's. Come on." He worked his way through the crowd, shaking hands and shouting questions into ears. Finally a stocky guy told him, "Sure, those two guys, there," and pointed toward the curve in the bar. Two men in uniform were deep in conversation. One wore sergeant's chevrons.

I put my hand on Marcolina's shoulder and went ahead of him toward the two. "Excuse me, fellows, Dave Williamson, Major Crimes. I need some help." I shook hands with both of them.

The sergeant's nametag read Bradley. He said, "Hi. What's going on?" He sounded tired or drunk, or both, and took a swallow from a bottle of Coors.

"I'm not sure what to do, here. We're working a little while ago, and we hear a call go out for an accident that's a block and a half from us, so we take it in. This guy, he's in bad shape from the wreck, but he's drunk off his ass. I can smell it coming out of his pores. I'm trying to check him out, see how bad he is, and he's carrying. I take a look in his wallet, and here, he's a Sheriff's Deputy, a sergeant." Bradley nodded and looked at the other guy. I continued, "I grabbed his stuff, you know, his badge and gun and all, cause I don't want him getting wrapped up, you know, with the job, and all. I did my best to tell him to keep his mouth shut. He was barely conscious, but I think he got it. But now – now I'm not sure I did the right thing, you know, so I wanted to talk to somebody that might know him."

"Who is he?"

"Dougherty. Joseph Dougherty."

The sheriffs looked at each other again and Bradley said, "Why don't we get away from this noise, so we don't have to shout at each other, okay?" He looked around the place and said, "Let's go outside. I wanna grab a smoke."

I nodded, and pushed my way through the bar and outside, with Bradley and Marcolina following me. We walked away from the entrance. Bradley lit up and said, "Sorry about the guy that got killed tonight. Retired, wasn't he?"

I said, "Yeah."

"You know him?"

"Yeah. He was a friend."

"That's rough. Sorry. Look," he continued, "look, I appreciate you watching out for a guy on the job. I just wish that, maybe with Dougherty, well, I wish maybe you hadn't come along, there."

I did my best to look confused. "Why? What's the matter?"

He hesitated and said, "Dougherty's a bad player."

"Aw, really?"

"Yeah, he's a load." Bradley took a drag. "Dougherty ran scared from day one. Prisoners had his number right away. None of the other deputies wanted to work with him, after they caught his act. He has drag, though. Got himself out of prisoner transport."

"He said something about working warrants."

"He's full of shit. He's used his connections to get some overtime with the unit. Went out with them a couple times, a while ago. Showed everybody he's a stiff. Finally, their commander told the boss no more. No, Dougherty does paperwork. Foreclosures, mostly." He spit tobacco off is lip. "But look, man, you did a good thing, there. It's not your fault the guy's an asshole. Thank you." He shook my hand again.

It was coming into focus. I said, "It looked like he was doing pretty well for himself on deputy sheriff's pay. You know, his car, his clothes."

Bradley hesitated, looked at Marcolina and said, "Where did you guys say you worked?"

Marcolina put up a hand. "No, no. This isn't anything like that. Honest."

I said, "This has nothing to do with us. I'm just curious."

Bradley smoked some more and said, "Dougherty's one of these dumb guys that's positive he's smarter than everybody else, okay? He's just smart enough to get himself in real trouble, someday. There are a lot of ways that a guy in his position can make money, if he wants to. Dougherty thinks that he came up with a few of these all on his own, but they've all been done before, and anybody who knows what they are can see them a mile away."

I said, "Just for my own knowledge, what does he do?"

He looked at Marcolina, back to me and said, "You got people, like, people that owe on their real estate tax. Eventually they're gonna lose their homes to the city. They can put this off for a while, make deals, payment plans, right? At the same time, there are speculators out there, looking to buy up property on the cheap and then flip."

I said, "So, Dougherty gives the speculator names and addresses?"

"Yeah, but there's nothing wrong with that. Anybody can find that stuff out if they look. As long as a guy like Dougherty doesn't take any money for it, there's no crime. In fact, the city prefers it. These people go to settlement, they get something out of the sale and the city gets their back taxes right there, plus, maybe now the city's got a property owner that keeps up with their responsibilities. Right?"

"So Dougherty gets something under the table?"

"Maybe. And maybe he helps things along, you know, he knocks on the people's door, scares them, tells them he's gonna foreclose on them, so they better sell while they can."

Marcolina said, "Yeah, but there couldn't be a lot of money in that, could there?"

"No," Bradley took another drag and said, "there wouldn't, and it would be hard to prove, anyway." Smoke jetted out of his mouth as he spoke. He watched traffic. "The thing is, when there is a sheriff's sale, there's almost always something left for the original owner, after they've satisfied back tax bills and any liens. But, this is Philadelphia, and processing is slow. So slow that lots of times the original owners die before it's all finished."

I said, "Get out."

"No. It happens more than you would think."

Marcolina said, "That makes sense. A lot of elderly people can't pay their real estate taxes."

Bradley pointed his finger at Marcolina like a pistol and said, "There you go. When those people die, the money is supposed to go to relatives, or it escheats – it goes to the state." He let us think about that for a moment and said, "Sometimes that money disappears."

I could see it. "It might be tough to keep track of all that, wouldn't it?"

Bradley said, "It could. Somebody would have to be looking for it, but it would be tough." He took one last drag and flipped away the smoke. "I'm not saying that's what Dougherty does, but he works where it's possible, and he is an asshole."

I said, "Thanks," and held out my hand.

Bradley took it and said, "Gimme his badge and gun. I'll take care of it for you."

I improvised. "My partner has it all. He's there at the hospital, still."

Bradley held on to my hand. "Wait – your partner?" He looked over at Marcolina, and said, "Then who are you?"

Marcolina put his hand out, "I'm Mister Dougherty's attorney —"

Bradley pushed himself away from me. "You pricks —"

Marcolina said, "Sergeant, you don't want to do anything that you'll regret."

Bradley looked at us both, turned and walked back inside the hall.

Marcolina watched him go, and turned to me and said, "Is that really your name? Dave Williamson?"

I walked toward Marcolina's car. "If Dougherty was taking the money that guy was talking about, it could be big."

Marcolina caught up and said, "Yeah, but he couldn't do it much without somebody getting wise. Everybody working for the city isn't stupid."

"Maybe somebody was making it all right."

"Who? Vic Pastore?"

"Why not. That could be why Dougherty is interested in what's in the safe."

"Wait. How do you know Dougherty?"

"Don't worry about it."

We got into the car and pulled away. Marcolina said, "Hey, that was good, you know, me and you working that guy, don't you think."

"Yeah. You were great."

12

We drove through the city toward the woman's neighborhood. Marcolina went on, talking about what he had planned for his share of the money in the safe when we found it. I tuned him out. I was considering the next few moves. Finally, I said, "Tell me about Brenda Michaels."

"What do you want to know?" He sounded hesitant – proprietary.

"What she does, where she works, what she looks like. Everything you know. For a start, how old is she?"

He relaxed a little. "I guess mid to late thirties. She might be forty. Looks good, though. Blonde, good build."

We pulled past her apartment house. It was a middle of the row, a four-story townhouse, twenty feet wide and eighty feet deep. I took a space in front of a driveway. As Marcolina began to protest I said, "We won't be long."

The front door opened into a vestibule with mailboxes and doorbells for the tenants. The door beyond that was the kind that allowed visitors to be buzzed in, and couldn't be dead-bolted. That was good, and I liked a place with a vestibule. The biggest problem with picking a lock is that you look like a guy picking a lock. I took out my tools and went to work.

Marcolina fretted, alternately looking out the front door window at his car, and over my shoulder. I said, "Relax. You're drawing attention." He did his best. I got us inside in a few seconds.

Her apartment was on the second floor, and was more difficult to get into; I had to pick the dead bolt and the knob. I put my gloves back on and opened the door. "Have you ever been inside this apartment?"

"No.

"Then put your hands in your pockets."

"Huh? Why?"

"That way you won't touch anything."

"Oh, yeah. Right, right." He did.

Inside, the apartment was done in earth tones, with the typical single women's touches – little pillows on the sofa and framed pictures of family and friends on little tables. I wanted to know what she looked like, and pointed to the photos. "Are any of these her?"

Marcolina studied them and pointed with his elbow to a picture of a blonde haired woman along with a young guy wearing Marine Corps dress blues. "That's her. A few years ago, anyway."

"Who's the grunt?"

"That's her little brother. Not the brother I know."

I kept looking around the living room. I saw that she was a reader; there were shelves full of books, mostly romance novels and bad self-help – the power of positive thinking crap. I pulled one off the shelf and paged through it; it was full of advice that all seemed to boil down to "visualizing your future."

Marcolina said, "I could probably be more help if I knew what we were looking for."

"I'm not sure myself. I'll know it when I see it."

He nodded. "Right, right."

We went into her kitchen. Her landlord had put money into it – the appliances were all new and expensive, and the cabinets were solid wood. She had put money into the kitchen, too; there were pieces of blue and orange enamel Le Creuset cookware hung from an iron rack, and a set of Wusthof knives in its wooden block stood on the countertop next to a white Kitchen Aid mixer – all of these apparently unused. There was no evidence that this woman had ever cooked a meal for herself. She had some packages of frozen stuff in the freezer, and left over take-out in the refrigerator. Other than some condiments and a bottle of wine, there was not much else.

There were a few notes and pictures stuck to the face of the refrigerator with funny magnets. Brenda was in two of the photos: one was of her with three other women, seated at a table in a club. The four of them were holding drinks and smiling at the camera. In the second, she stood with Pastore on the deck of his boat. She wore a blue, two-piece bathing suit, and appeared to be laughing at something he'd said. He wore a tee shirt and trunks, and stood there with his arm around her waist. In another photo were three guys wearing desert camouflage and day-glow yellow traffic vests, armed, standing in front of a gate, at an air base somewhere in the Middle East. I tapped on the photo and said, "What about the brother? Is he still in the Corps?"

"No." Marcolina shook his head. "No, he had some problems."

"Post Traumatic Stress?"

"Hardly. He was enjoying himself a little too much. He worked prisoner transport. He liked to rough them up. Carried a pair of pliers with him, if you catch my drift."

"How do you know any of this?"

"He told a few guys at the club some stuff. Other things you hear around, you know? Something happened to some Iraqi guy – a guy that turned out to be somebody. There was an investigation. The brass wanted to court-martial him. Boot him out with a B.C.D."

"Did they?"

"Nah, their family's got an uncle who's somebody big in the Ironworker's local, and he's tight with a congressman. He said something to somebody at the Pentagon, and it all went away – the kid got out with a General Under Honorable Conditions. Like everything else, it's all who you know."

A calendar was tacked to the wall. Yesterday's date had a star drawn on it in pen and crossed out. Tonight's date had two stars drawn across it. I looked over at Marcolina; he was wandering around the apartment, taking it all in. He'd never been inside before. It was clear to me that this woman had Marcolina whipped. I said, "Hey. What does this mean?" and tapped the calendar.

He looked and said, "You got me. I mean, the one star could mean, it could be the thing, you know, that you were doing with George, but I don't know what else she could – I don't know what it means."

The desk in her middle room had some paper work and hand written notes on its top but none yielded anything useful. Her computer wouldn't, either. There was a journal in the drawer –

mostly nonsense about men, work and girlfriends she didn't really like – nothing that helped.

In the top, side drawer was a black marble notebook. Inside, the pages were divided into neat columns: the first were names of businesses – they seemed mostly restaurants, the second a first name and a phone number, the third a number, mostly ones or twos, but occasionally larger; there was an eight and a fifteen. Some of these had a check mark next to it. A lot of the entries were crossed out with a single line, and if so, included a date and the circled letters 'PIF.' – probably 'paid in full.' Two of the business names were crossed out with a series of X's, drawn in red ink. Both of these were in Chinatown.

There was a locked two-drawer file cabinet in the corner of the room. Inside the bottom drawer were file folders filled with correspondence loaded with legalese, and personal stuff, labeled "Insurance, Medical" and other things like that. The top drawer contained a small, gray steel strongbox. It sat on top of more black marble notebooks. I said to Marcolina, "What was that?"

"What?"

"I heard someone coming into the building. Turn out the lights. Use this," I gave him my handkerchief. "Listen by the door – quietly."

He nodded and tip-toed out of the room, and I opened the box. Inside was a wad of cash, in different denominations – at least fifteen hundred dollars. I stuck it all in my pocket and looked at the notebooks.

The first two were improvised ledger books like the one in her desk. The rest all seemed to contain college essays, rough drafts written in pencil, on a variety of subjects: the WPA during the Great Depression; a book report of *Their Eyes Were Watching God*; a critique debunking supply-side economics, and other things like that, all written for a variety of classes, and all attributed to different students.

I locked the cabinet, walked into the woman's bedroom and began going through her closet. Her things weren't cheap.

Marcolina crept to the bedroom door, saw me and whispered, "I don't hear anything out in the hall." He gave back the handkerchief.

"Good. It must have been something outside." This woman had a lot of nice things to wear, but nothing in the closet helped me. "What does Brenda like to do on a Friday night? Does she have a boyfriend?" Dozens of pairs of shoes and fancy boots littered the floor. I turned the boots over and shook them; there was nothing hidden in them.

Marcolina stood in the doorway, reluctant to be part of this violation of privacy. "Well, no, not really, nobody that she sees on any regular —"

"How about guys that she doesn't see regularly?"

He didn't seem to like thinking about it. "I don't know."

The closet shelf held a hatbox, some bedding and an old portable Olivetti typewriter in avocado green. The hatbox had a hat inside it. I moved to her bureau. "Where does she go at night?"

"She kind of hangs around a few places." Out of habit I pulled open the bottom drawer first. Marcolina said, "Hey, you shouldn't –"

I looked up, annoyed. "Do you know what we're doing here? We need to find this woman, quickly. Right now. We want to find the money. Understand?"

"Yeah, yeah." He got himself under control. I went through the rest of the drawers. There was nothing hidden, nothing to help.

This was a nice apartment, in a nice neighborhood. This woman shouldn't need money. Either she had a problem that wasn't immediately apparent, or she was in this to make trouble for Pastore. Either reason bothered me. It wasn't professional.

I stood and repeated, "Where does she go at night?"

"The thing is, Brenda's popular. She's got a lot of friends. There are lots of places she could be."

"Ok, if you wanted to find her tonight, 'just to hang out,' where would you try?"

He reddened. "Last week she mentioned this new club in Fishtown that she wanted to check out."

I looked around while I thought it over. There was no reason to tear this place apart. It was unlikely that there was anything to help me and also unlikely a woman like this would have more cash – that she had any at all surprised me. She worked for a firm that would direct deposit her salary, and she would pay for things with a card, when she had to. I said, "Ok. Let's go there."

In the hallway, I shut the door behind us and set about locking the deadbolt. Marcolina watched and said, "I never thought about that. Is it hard to do?"

I don't care for idle chatter, but it seems to keep people calm, and can make them easier to handle. I needed to keep Marcolina invested in this effort. I worked at the lock for a few seconds and said, "This came open pretty easily but it's tough to get locked again. That's how it goes. Sometimes the cylinder moves more easily in one direction than the other." There was a *snap* as the lock engaged. I stood and put away the picks. "There's a tool that locks them back up once you've picked them — it's spring-loaded," I took off the gloves, "but I don't have one."

There was a ticket under his wiper. I handed it to him as I settled into the driver's seat. He didn't say anything, just put it in the glove compartment.

I pulled away from the curb and said, "What do you know about Vic Pastore?"

"Probably no more than anyone else. What do you want to know?"

That was a good question. I wasn't sure. I wanted to know where the safe was. I said, "I'm just trying to get a sense of the man."

Marcolina was quiet for a few moments, and said, "The thing about Vic Pastore is the same thing about all these guys – connections are everything. He's made himself into the guy that you call to straighten something out, get yourself out of a jam, you know? He makes friends. He's the guy you call to get your street paved, or to get a ticket fixed."

"He's a lawyer, right? How about his law practice?"

"What practice? The only time he uses the law degree is in real estate deals. I heard even then he's a hack. His old man wanted him to be a lawyer, so he's a lawyer. That's how he's always operated. His father paid his way through St. Joe's and Penn Law, and paid Reilly to do all Vic's work for him. The word around the courts is that Reilly took the bar exam for him too, after he'd flunked it twice."

"What about Reilly? What's his deal?"

"Reilly's smart. He's a Fishtown boy who went to The Prep on a scholarship. Pastore took a shine to him, or Reilly sucked up. Or both. One way or the other, they started to hang out and never quit. He's got asthma, I think. I saw him have an episode of some kind at the courthouse a couple years ago. Ambulance had to come for him. Nobody likes him, but I still kind of felt bad for the guy, you know? Just imagine not being able to breathe."

We drove out to Delaware Avenue and diagonalled left onto Frankford. This close to Center City it was a narrow two-lane commercial artery. Most of the buildings here were undistinguished and unimpressive – either vacant or just uncared for. A few blocks beyond that were some lights and foot traffic. "The club's a little farther," Marcolina said, "it's up ahead, past St. Mary's." We cruised by the old hospital, and a couple blocks later, he said, "There it is. Park anywhere you can." In front of a row of darkened buildings stood a dozen or so people.

"That doesn't look like a club to me."

"It's a speakeasy. It's the new thing, man. These places are really popular."

I found a spot and parked. A breeze swirled trash on the street. The people waiting in line were overdressed for the neighborhood. I pushed my way past the couple in front. The woman said something I ignored. The steel security door was swung open and hooked to the front wall. Hung behind that and barring entrance was a fancy wrought iron security grate, it's design vaguely Asian. A big, bored-looking guy stood, leaning against the wall of the stairwell. He was playing with something on his phone. I said, "Hey."

The bouncer made a point of not paying attention for a few seconds while he did something on the phone and said, "What?" He looked up slowly.

I showed him the badge. "Let us in."

He frowned and came close, squinting at the ID. "Where'd you get that? A cereal box?

"Sheriff's. Open up."

"I don't know. I gotta call upstairs."

"You're not going to call anybody. You're going to do what I said."

He looked down at the phone in his hand and back and said, "Let me see that." He reached through the grate for the ID.

I grabbed his hand and yanked his arm through. His head slammed into the grate. The phone clattered on the floor. "Ow! What the fuck, man?" He struggled to grab my hand.

I twisted the bouncer's arm and bent his fingers backward. The big man whined and gave up. I spoke quietly. "You've just committed a felony. Open up."

The man reached for the key ring and struggled one-handed to unlock the grate. The people in line scattered, hurrying away in all directions. Marcolina was standing with his mouth open. I looked back at the bouncer. His eyes were watering. When he got the door opened it swung inward, toward him. I stepped inside and pinned the doorman between the grate and the wall. "Put your other hand through." I cuffed him, and took his keys.

The bouncer said, "Aw, come on, man."

Marcolina was still standing there. I said, "Let's go. Close the front door behind us." I stomped the bouncer's phone. The glass crackled under my sole.

"Yo!"

"Shut up." We went up the stairs.

The club was doing well but wasn't over-crowded; I supposed that's what the gorilla downstairs was for. The walls were the color of Chinese eggplant. The bar was mahogany. It all had a sort of Art Nouveau look. Music played over the sound system, but not so loudly that conversation was impossible. I turned to Marcolina. "Where is she?"

"I don't see her. Let me look around some more."

We walked through the place. I went to the bar for a glass of water. The night was catching up with me. I took out Tom's pills and washed down two.

Marcolina spotted a guy and said, "There's a friend of hers. Hey, Larry!"

A tall, thin man, who appeared to be in his thirties turned around, and recognizing Marcolina, smiled and fluttered his fingers at him. He had a drink in the other hand. He came toward us, and spoke to Marcolina while he stared at me. He said, "Mickey, how are you? I haven't seen you, lately. First time here?"

"Yeah." Marcolina nodded to me and said, "My friend and I are – "

"Oh, you have a friend now? How perfect."

"Come on, Larry." He made a face and tried again. "We're looking for Brenda. Have you seen her?"

To me, Larry said, "Mickey knows I love to tease. How about you, friend? What's your deal?"

"I need to talk to Brenda Michaels. Do you know where we can find her?"

"That all depends on whether or not Brenda wants to be found. I don't think she would want you to find her. No offense, but you're definitely not her type. What do you think, Mickey?"

"No, this is about something she wants to happen."

Larry looked back. I said, "It's all good. She'll want to talk to me."

"I'm not so sure. Why don't we have a drink and talk about this a little. Do you have a name, friend?"

"Yeah, but friend will work for now. I'll have a drink with you while you tell us where she is."

"All right, monorail mind. She went to a house party in Germantown." He finished his drink and put it on the bar. "I was thinking about going there myself." "Good. You can come with us." I took his elbow and started to lead him out of the club.

Larry said, "Wait, wait, I have to tell—"

"You can call them from the car."

We all went down the stairs. Larry saw the bouncer manacled to the grate and said, "Oh, I don't know about this." I tightened my grip on Larry's arm and propelled him ahead. Larry turned to Marcolina. "What's going on?"

"It's all right. Don't worry about it."

I uncuffed the bouncer. The man rubbed his wrists and said, "You didn't have to break my phone, man."

"I know."

I had Larry ride shotgun and got behind the wheel. Larry said, "Mickey, why is this man driving your car?"

Marcolina improvised. "Suspended license."

He got into the back seat and we took the Vine Street Expressway through Center City and onto the East River Drive. We passed Boathouse Row. The Schuylkill River was on our left as we traveled toward the Northwest part of the city. Gusts tossed the leaves on the trees. Lightning flashed silently in the distance. Marcolina and Larry chatted until I said, "Who is Brenda's type?"

Larry said, "Pardon?"

"You said that I wasn't her type. I want to know who is."

"Oh." Larry thought for a moment. "The best way to put it? Mostly, she likes rich assholes. Brenda's a sweetie-pie, but she's got a mercenary streak when it comes to boyfriends."

"Who else?"

"Pardon?"

I was growing weary of Larry. "You said that 'mostly' she dated rich assholes. Who else?"

"So, I did. Well, every now and then, Brenda goes slumming. Last week I saw her at Continental with a fellow whom I would tend to describe as rough. Hmm." I turned to look at him. He was staring, appraising me in an amused way, and said, "Perhaps I spoke too soon, friend. You may have a chance." He turned in his seat and said to Marcolina, "Don't fret. That fellow I saw Brenda with? It won't last."

Marcolina was sulky. "None of my business."

I said, "Who's going to be at this party?"

"Oh, there will be all kinds at this soiree. Diverse. Gabriel throws the very best parties." He chuckled, "This is a 'Halloween in Spring' party. Gabriel just loves Halloween. Do we have time to shop for costumes?"

"No."

13

We made our way around a crew resurfacing the roadway, and took Lincoln Drive, paralleling the Wissahickon Creek through the park. Larry had me turn up a hill, through the neighborhood, to Wayne Avenue, and right onto a tree-lined street of big twins and singles. Three blocks in, Larry said, "There it is, up on the right. Park anywhere you can." It was a huge three-story, stone Victorian, with lots of windows and gingerbread. I U-turned and took a spot across the street, three houses down. In the rearview I saw the sky behind us light up again

We piled out of the car. The house was set back from the street. Music from a stereo was loud even out there on the sidewalk. Some of the partygoers were outdoors, smoking in the driveway, a few in costume. A Raggedy Anne and Raggedy Andy were sharing a joint. We went past them, nodding, and inside. The main entrance was on the side of the house.

It felt fifteen degrees hotter inside. Larry scanned the crowd, screamed, "Darling!" and ran to a woman with bright red hair. She was dressed in a cat suit and sported a black nose and whiskers. They joined hands, put their faces near each other and kissed the air. Marcolina and I went past them into the living room. It was jammed. A Scarecrow and Dorothy walked by, but only a few guests were in costume; most had skipped dressing up. Larry hadn't exaggerated. There were all kinds. Marcolina said, "I don't see her. Maybe the kitchen."

We made our way through the first floor hallway. The kitchen was big, twenty-five feet deep and a dozen wide. Food in bowls and on plates covered the table and counter tops. A bald guy in his forties with a bushy beard, and wearing black tights, bee's wings and antennae came up to us and said, "Help yourselves to something to eat. There're all sorts of things here – two kinds of chili, one with meat and one vegan, both are delicious. Lots of salads," he pointed to a platter on the countertop, " and that humus is very tasty. The beverages are all in the dining room." He smiled at me and said, "I know you, don't I? Don't you teach at Temple?" He touched my forearm.

I smiled and said, "Not this semester." Before he could ask me something else, I said, "I was supposed to meet Brenda Michaels here. Have you seen her?"

"Yes, yes, I don't know where she is, but she's around here, somewhere." He tried again, "I think I met you at a workshop last year. Maybe?"

"Maybe."

Two men came in through the side door. One spoke to the bee. "Benjamin, how are you?"

Benjamin smiled, touched my arm again, and moved over to them. I grabbed Marcolina and said, "Let's keep looking." He scooped some hummus with a chip and came along.

In the hallway, a tall black man wearing a Frankenstein monster costume complete with bolts stopped in front of us and said, "I don't believe that we've met."

"No," I gave him a name and extended my hand.

He smiled and took my hand, and said, "That's not quite sufficient. How is it that you're here?"

"I'm a friend of Benjamin's and Larry's. What about you?"

"I'm the host. My name is Gabriel."

"Oh, of course. It's a pleasure to meet you," I turned to Marcolina and said, "And this is my friend, Mickey."

Marcolina waved and said, "Hi."

"Charmed." He gave my hand another squeeze and said, "Enjoy," and walked past us.

We found her in the dining room. She didn't look like she had in the photo with her brother, but was more what Marcolina had described: blonde, attractive, taller than him, but not too tall. She wore a tight, black dress, and was talking to two other women, also tall and good-looking, while she sent a text message. The three of them were the sort of women who knew their looks were their best assets. Brenda was different than the other two, though. There was something about her face, or maybe the way she held herself that conveyed a feeling of bitterness. This was a woman who felt she'd been cheated.

None of the women were looking at each other. They continuously surveyed the crowd, making only the briefest eye contact with each other and nodding, while they spoke. Brenda saw Marcolina coming near her and kept right on talking, never missing a beat.

When Marcolina got close, he said, "Excuse me, ladies. Brenda, hi. We have to talk. About that thing, you know?"

She put away her phone and spoke to Marcolina while looking at me, "I'm surprised to see you here. I didn't know that you and Gabe were friends."

Marcolina said, "We're not. I have to talk to you about that thing."

"Yeah, you said. All right, let's get you both a drink and we'll sit down somewhere and talk."

The other women looked at us, and one said, "I'm thinking about trying that party in East Falls." She looked at me and said, "There aren't many straight men here." She spoke to Brenda, "Let me know if you want a ride." The two of them moved away.

I told Marcolina, "Wait here," and took Brenda by the arm and led her toward the stairway. "We'll skip the drinks."

"Whoa." She tried to pull free. "Who the hell are you?"

Marcolina followed us and said, "It's all right. This is, well, you should talk to him."

She started to speak, but I kept moving her toward the stairs and said quietly, "These next few minutes are very important, so you don't want to make a mistake."

She said, "You sound serious."

"I'm the most serious man you will ever meet."

"Okay, okay. Listen to me," she stopped and looked me over, "you have to at least try to fit in here. I work with some of these people. Let me get you a drink. You can just hold it if you don't want it. Okay?"

I was thirsty. "All right."

She took my arm and said, "You're not what I expected." There was nothing for me to say to that. We walked into the dining room. There was an assortment of bottles on a table that had been pushed up against the wall. I let her fix me a seltzer with ice and a wedge of lime. She steered me toward the steps and said, "Now try to look like you're here to have a good time."

A black couple passed us, coming down. I smiled at them, like I was here to have a good time. It was hotter upstairs. Save a couple waiting to use the bathroom, the second floor was empty. I moved us into an empty room.

She sat on the bed. "I suppose something went wrong?"

"Badly." It was stifling in the room. I tried to raise the window, but it was painted shut. Lightning flashed again, closer this time; a few seconds later a low rumble sounded.

There was a letter desk against the wall. I pulled the chair out and sat down, facing her. "We were hijacked. My partner in this is dead."

She tried not to react, but did – she was visibly upset. I doubted that she was faking. She began twice to say something, but stopped and blessed herself; the motion seemed more automatic than heartfelt.

I said, "Who are the guys in the red van?"

"I have no idea," she said. "What van?"

"Who else knew about this?"

"Nobody." She said this too quickly, and I could see that she realized it. She was conscious of herself. "Not at least as far as I know." She got herself under control and said, "Ask Mickey."

"I already have. I want to hear it from you."

She changed the subject. "How much money was there?"

I ignored her question and said, "Somebody knew."

"That could be, but nobody heard about it from me." I made to speak, but she continued, "Look, I wanted this to work. I want the money." She tried again. "Was there a lot?"

"I'm here to ask questions, not answer them." She looked annoyed. I thought about it; she was in the same position as George's wife – it didn't make sense for her to be in this with somebody else. Besides, in Brenda's case, if she knew another thief, why go to Marcolina?

She might be more helpful if I gave a little. "I don't know how much money there was."

"But there was money, right?"

"No idea."

"Didn't you open the safe?" I shook my head no. She said, "Why would somebody try to kill you if it wasn't open?"

"I stole the safe." I took a sip of my drink. "We hadn't opened it yet."

"Oh. Why wouldn't you –"

"We don't have time for this. Who would Pastore have looking out for him, protecting him?"

"That's easy." She rolled her eyes. "His best friend in the whole wide world, Eddie Reilly." She looked disgusted and added, "That little weasel."

"From what everyone says, Reilly's flown the coop."

"I don't know what else to tell you. Eddie's his man. That's who would be looking out for him."

"Ok, what about you?"

"What's that supposed to mean?"

A woman opened the door, saw us and said, "Sorry," and closed it again.

Brenda looked back at me and said, again, "What's that supposed to mean? 'What about me?'"

"I mean, tell me about Pastore – you and him."

"There's not much there. We dated for a little while."

"Why'd he break up with you?"

"Who says he broke up with me?"

"You did. That's what you told Mickey, anyway."

"I tell Mickey a lot of things." She made eyes at me. I didn't react, and she said, "But, yeah, you're right. He broke it off with me."

I waited and said, "I'm getting tired of asking you the same questions twice. Why?"

She frowned at me and said, "He tried me on for size and I didn't fit." It sounded like the kind of line she had rehearsed. She must have sensed my impatience, and said, "Look, it was never really serious. We had fun for a little while, and then we – he – moved on. Okay?"

"No." I took the key to his front door out of my pocket and held it up. "This key says that he was doing more than having fun for a while."

"Don't read too much into that key. He gave it to me so he wouldn't have to come and pick me up." Thinking about this made her angry. She was smart, and as Larry had said, she was mercenary – disappointments upset her, and it showed. "He told me he didn't have time to come get me. Very big man. Very busy guy." She gestured toward the key in my hand. "Believe me, I never gave him mine."

"So this whole thing is just a fuck you to Pastore?"

"What? No. I want the money."

A couple burst into the room, giggling. The man had a hand on the woman's ass. She gave a little scream when she saw us. The man said, "Oh. I didn't know this was occupied."

I said, "It is." They left, leaving the door ajar and went giggling down the hall.

I turned back to Brenda, "Why?"

She gave me a blank look.

"The money. Why do you want it?"

"Why not?"

"Because your end wouldn't be that much." She started to speak and I said, "I didn't believe that half a million dollar story of yours for a second, but even if there was a lot of money, your end wouldn't be much. And then I look at you, and I have to ask myself, does this woman, this very smart woman, really want to get herself involved in a major crime, a felony, for a few bucks?" I let her think for a few moments and said, "What's really going on?"

She stuck to it. "There's money in that safe. A lot."

"I heard tonight that he's been having money troubles."

She was stubborn. "No. He has money."

"I'm a thief. Didn't it occur to you that I'd probably rip you off?"

It hadn't. She said, "You wouldn't have to – I mean, we didn't –" She stopped, took a few seconds and said, "My girlfriends from school all married guys from Saint Rita's and live in row houses with their husbands and children. I never wanted that. I went to college for a year, but my mother died and I had to drop out. I'm a legal secretary at a good firm. I get paid pretty well, and I live in a nice place, but it's an apartment. I'm tired of paying rent, contributing to someone else's fortune. I want to live in a house, my own house, okay? I saw this as a way to get a nice down payment."

I thought about the notebook in her desk drawer. "You're a legal secretary?"

She nodded.

"What else?"

"What do you mean?"

I didn't want to give anything away. I said, "Do you do any other work? Anything to make a few extra bucks?"

"There is no such thing as extra money." She looked at me, thinking, and said, "Yes, I do bookkeeping for some small businesses. Local places. I've been doing it since high school. Why?"

"No reason."

Someone else moved in the hallway. More were in line for the bathroom. It seemed noticeably hotter in the room. "Ok." I looked at Brenda; I didn't care about cheering her up. I tossed down the rest of the seltzer and said, "What else do you know about Pastore that could help?"

"I don't know."

I thought for a moment and said, "What about his boat? He put it in somebody else's name."

She looked at her nails. "I don't know anything about that."

"He seems to like that boat a lot. I'd think to be his girlfriend you'd have to like it too."

She said, "Not me. I get seasick." That bothered me, but I wasn't sure why. She wrinkled her nose, and added, "He likes it."

"Yeah, that's what I said."

"No, really," she licked her lips, and trailed her fingers down her torso. "I mean he likes it more than most things."

"You're annoying me."

"Sorry." She bit her lip. "I'm trying to tell you that he's a strange guy. He likes to have a pretty girl around, but that's all."

"He doesn't have sex?"

She shook her head. "He didn't with me. I know another woman that he dated a few years ago, and he didn't with her either."

"Is he queer?"

She smiled and looked at the line in the hallway for the bathroom, and back at me and said, "You need be more up to date, especially in this house. 'Queer' is not the appropriate term anymore."

"Really? I thought it was."

"Not the way you say it. It's all in the delivery. No, I don't think that Vic is gay. I think he's asexual. Just no real interest."

"Who's your boyfriend now?"

She stretched and smiled again. "I'm currently available."

"That's not what Larry says."

"Well, isn't Larry the chatterbox? The gentleman he saw me with last week doesn't count."

"Where is he? Why isn't he here?"

She laughed at that. "This sort of party wouldn't be his cup of tea. Besides, he's working." She sobered for a moment, and added, "I'm not looking for anything serious. I stopped waiting for Mister Wonderful to come along a long time ago. It's always too sad when you get to the end of someone – when you've been with them long enough to learn that that's all they are."

Steps pounded up the stairs. Marcolina went past the door, pushing his way through the crowd in the hallway, and started up the flight to the third floor. The two hard guys went up after him.

14

I told Brenda, "Wait here," and went out into the hallway. I could hear the two catch up with Marcolina upstairs. I cut in front of a man in line and forced open the bathroom door, breaking the hasp. A woman sitting on the toilet screamed and covered her face. I said, "Sorry," grabbed a hand towel and pushed past the guy in the hall. I pulled Dougherty's gun and wrapped the towel around the barrel as I took the stairs to the third floor.

The party hadn't made it up here yet; the music could still be heard, but not as loudly. They were all in the front room. The two were giving Marcolina a hard way to go. One of them had twisted Marcolina's arm behind his back. The other said, "You better not be wasting our time." Again, he sounded Eastern European.

I stepped into the room and pointed the pistol at them. "Quit it, now."

They faced me. The one holding Marcolina let him go, looked at me, back at Marcolina, and smacked the back of his head. Marcolina said, "Ow!" and to me, "Thanks, man. I –"

"Shut up. Go out to the car and wait for me." He went past me and down the stairs.

One of the thugs said, "You can't shoot us both."

I pointed the gun at his face. "I'll shoot you, then." He smirked. Under his collar, on the right side of his neck, I could see a tattoo of a two-headed bird – the Albanian national emblem. "You two work for Mr. Anton."

The first guy looked at the other and said, "No fucking way. We work for no one."

"Then why are you bothering Marcolina?"

"He owes us money."

I was losing patience with their lack of candor, and let it show on my face. "Explain."

"We buy his debt from Anton."

"Why are you bothering him here, now?"

The second guy pointed at the floor. "Is where we find him."

"Why the full-court press?"

He was confused by the basketball analogy. The other guy said, "He made us promise." Through the window, I saw Marcolina, Larry and Brenda run out to the sidewalk and toward the car. Thunder sounded.

The first guy looked annoyed and said something to him in what I supposed was Albanian. The other answered. Then they were arguing, talking over each other.

I saw movement in the street below. Marcolina drove back the way we came. I cursed under my breath. He must have had another key.

The Albanians kept it up. I said, "Stop."

They did, and stared at me.

I bluffed. "What do you two want with Pastore's papers?" That was it. They both reacted to the name. I took out the cuffs and tossed them to the second guy. "Your wrist." And tapped mine. He tried a few faces, doing his best to look hard for a few moments, but began to put it on his left wrist. "No. The other." He snapped it onto his right. I said to the first, "Your right ankle."

"No fucking way. Who do you think you're fucking with?" He took a step toward me. I fired a round past his ear. The bullet punched through the plaster behind him. The towel muffled the shot only a little. He stopped, and for a moment lost his composure. I pointed the gun back at his face. He said, "Peoples downstairs – they heard that – they call police."

"No. They'll think it's the storm."

He frowned and pulled the other guy's arm across and down and closed the loose cuff around his right ankle. Through the music and the ringing in my ears, I heard footsteps on the stairs behind me, heavy – a man's

The thugs were facing in opposite directions, the second guy bent over, to accommodate the short handcuff chain. The first guy said something else in Albanian and reached behind him.

"Hey." I moved the gun around enough to make him stop. "Sit." He did.

The heavy footsteps gained the top of the stairway and came down the hall, toward us. I needed to get rid of him. Without turning, I said, "I'm a police officer. These men are in my custody. Go downstairs and call nine-one-one." The first guy's eyes showed something and went back to stone-faced.

The man behind me said, "All right." I heard the Urals in his voice. I launched myself backwards; his fist sailed past my ear as the back of my head crushed his nose. We kept going. I held tight to the gun; the towel fell away. We landed out in the hallway. He grunted, and the wind rushed out of his lungs, but he was tough, and tried to recover, wrapping his arms around me. His hand scrabbled around my face and I got his thumb between my teeth and bit down as hard as I could, while I chopped at his ribs with my elbow. The two lumbered toward us as best they could. I fired three shots over their heads; the rounds punched through the ceiling. Plaster dust fell. The two stopped. The guy was still fighting, hitting me in the ear with his free hand. I slammed the back of my head into his face again; his teeth came together with a *click,* and I felt him go limp under me. Downstairs, the music had stopped. My ears rang on.

I shook his hand away from my face, spit blood and shouted, "Enough. Sit down." They did. I kept the gun aimed at the pair, slid off the guy on the floor and stood, and dragged him up by his collar. He was barely conscious. I asked the two, "This is Anton?" They stared at me. I shook him. "You're Anton, right?" He didn't answer but opened his eyes to look at me. I took it as a yes and said, "Let's go." Blood ran from his ruined nose, dripping down onto his shirt. I could hear a siren, off in the distance.

I said to the two, "You ladies have a nice night," and shepherded Anton back down the stairs. He barely managed to stay upright, holding onto the railing two-handed. The siren sounded closer. Anton sagged against the banister and stopped. If he couldn't get it together, I'd have to leave him. I shook him again and said, "Listen." It seemed to register. "You don't want to stay around and talk to the police, do you?"

He shook his head and said, "No," and did a little better.

We passed a few people on the second floor. I held the pistol down, along my leg. No one noticed it; they were all staring at Anton's bloody face. One said, "What happened?" I ignored them and pushed Anton ahead of me.

Benjamin, the Bee, challenged us on the ground floor: "In this house, we do not solve our problems with violence."

Anton spit blood on the carpet, and said, "Blow it out your ass, mudder-fucker."

The siren was close. I steered Anton to the door and outside. It had started to drizzle. There were spots on the flagstone walk. "Where's your car?" He looked both ways, still dazed, trying to remember. I said, "Come on, think."

He pointed to the right at a green Volvo coupe, and said, "This way."

We trotted off toward it. The siren cut off. It sounded as though the cop was still a couple blocks away. I said, "Give me your keys."

"Fuck you. I will drive."

"Come on, you probably have a concussion."

He stopped alongside the car. " I will drive," he wiggled his fingers, "that way, you can watch my hands, yes?" Blood ran from his thumb down his wrist.

He seemed to be doing better. I decided to let him. "Yes." I made him unlock both doors and we got in together.

A patrol car turned onto the street, its light bar flashing. Anton said, "We wait until he goes inside."

I nodded. "Where's my safe?"

"I don't know what you talk of." He looked at his hand and said, "You almost bit my fucking thumb off." I didn't respond. He made to reach across me, but I stuck the muzzle against his throat. He said, "I've got towel in glove box. To wipe my face, asshole."

"Slowly."

"Okay, okay." He unlatched the box and took some tissues. "Sorry." Another police car turned onto the block. He watched it, and said, "I am a professional. I don't carry unless I need to." He adjusted the mirror to look at himself. "Ah!"

"You'll live."

The first cop got out of his car, putting on his hat and hunching his shoulders against the raindrops as he made his way toward the house.

Anton dabbed at his face, wiping off the blood, and said, "We go now, before any others show up." He sounded better. He steered around the police cars and turned onto McCallum Street. "This was new – a new – shirt." So, he'd been here long enough to understand some of the niceties of English speech, he just hadn't made them a habit yet. He glanced over at me, and seemingly read my mind. He looked back at the street and said, "That's right. I took ESL. Community College of Philadelphia," sounding out every syllable.

I repeated, "Where's my safe." In case he was confused, I added, "The one I took out of Pastore's house."

"Honestly, I don't know."

"You Albanian, too?"

"Fuck no. Pigs." He spit blood out the window. "I am Slovak."

I didn't recognize the distinction in class, but let it go. "What was all that about, back there?"

The rain fell harder. Anton turned on the wipers. "Marcolina owes me much money."

"No. You sold his debt to those two back there."

"Those two work for me."

"That's not what they say."

"Those two work for me." He sucked on the side of his thumb and spit out the window. "I let them think what they want. It makes guys like them easier to handle. Without me, they don't have nothing."

I didn't care about who worked for who. "Danny Raco isn't happy about your guys coming into his neighborhood without permission. You're stepping on the toes of a dangerous man."

"This is not Raco's business. Mickey owes me money. So. They go where they have to."

"How did they know he was at the party?"

"I get text message," he steered around a corner, "I call them."

"Who sent you the text?"

He hesitated and said, "A businessman, like me."

"You got a message from the guy in the red van?"

"I don't know what you talk of."

"Your businessman friend – does he drive a red van?"

"Why should I know what they are driving?"

I let it go for the time being. "All this is too much. You know where Marcolina lives, where he works. He's not going anywhere. You can put your hands on him any time you want." I let that sink in. ""What's really going on?"

He drove another block and said, "I expect him to get something for me."

"What?" He stayed quiet. I put my hands in my lap, letting the pistol show. "I'm getting tired of asking you questions."

"Okay, okay, I'll tell you," he nodded toward the gun, "put that thing away."

"No. I don't know you at all. You look like the kind of man who holds a grudge."

"I don't know 'grudge.'"

"You might stay angry with me."

"No. This with me and you, this was an understanding."

"Do you mean a misunderstanding?"

"Yes, yes, my mistake. A misunderstanding. Please, put away the gun. Come, we are both professionals."

"Yes, we are." I held on to it. "What was Marcolina supposed to get for you?"

Anton grimaced and said, "Okay, okay. Hold it if it makes you feel better."

"What was Marcolina supposed to get for you?"

He steered onto Walnut Lane. "Some paperwork. A book." Before I could voice my impatience, he said, "I help some people I know bring goods into the country. This is not easy – Homeland Security, Patriot Act – ships from overseas are checked very good." He slowed for a red light in the distance and resumed speed as it turned green. "There is a guy, a contractor. He meets ships while still out in the bay. Takes goods with him. Ship comes in to port clean."

"What's his name?"

"I don't know."

"Bullshit."

"No, no bullshit. I don't *want* to know his name." He glanced at me and said, "I also don't want to know your name."

I let that go. "This guy is using Pastore's boat, right."

"Ah, you have a good brain." Anton smiled. "It is good to deal with professional." He checked his rear view mirror.

We'd come to the Walnut Lane Circle. Anton steered around it and headed over the bridge to Roxborough. I didn't know this neighborhood that well. I knew that it was old, like Germantown, but built on the side of a hill, and it was mostly white, and mostly residential. There was some industry closer to the river.

It was raining hard now. "Where are you going?"

"We go downtown. Is nothing for us here." He anticipated my next question and said, "They work tonight on River Drive. We take expressway. Get on at Belmont Avenue. Fast way. No traffic." He steered around a downed tree limb in the roadway as we drove past the public golf course, and turned right onto Henry Avenue, a broad, four-lane street, and made a point of checking his rear view mirror again. We went past a hoagie shop and a bar.

I didn't trust him any more now just because he was acting friendly. I looked back at him and said, "Why is Pastore letting them use his boat?"

"Not my business."

"No, but you have an idea."

He sped up to make a light, and said, "I maybe think he doesn't want to." To our right now were thick woods. A lightning flash lit the road ahead of us, and the thunderclap seemed to rock the car. I blinked away the after-image. A median here split the roadway. Anton looked up at the rearview, and back to the road. "I maybe think he owes somebody. Who knows?" He sounded distracted

I pressed him. "But you think Pastore is keeping records about the boat? Records that could hurt you?"

"Yes. Maybe. I don't want to take chance?"

"Have you dealt with him directly?"

"No."

"Then how would he have your name on anything?" He didn't say anything. I continued, "Your actions here are way oversized. What else is going on?"

He looked over at me and said, "Somebody shoot cop tonight."

"Yeah, I know, but that just happened. You were running around before. What else?"

"Nothing."

I was annoyed. "I could shoot you and take this car into town. Or, you could be helpful."

"All right, all right. Something happen last night." Before I could interrupt, he said, "Don't ask. I don't know what, I don't care what. Trouble. Trouble for everybody. Lots of guys angry, lots of guys scared. I try to protect myself." He glanced my way. "Go ahead and shoot if that's not good enough."

He was lying, but seemed determined not to say more. He swerved again; there was a disabled car in the right lane. I looked back at him and it took a moment for my eyes to focus. I blinked and said, "What sort of 'goods' are you bringing in?"

"Not me. I don't bring in nothing."

"All right, not you. What are your associates dealing in?"

"How should I know? I am just a businessman." He turned left onto Leverington Avenue, away from the woods. There were fewer trees here; two and three-story houses lined the street. "I put people together and take my small profits. Everything else is not my business."

I didn't believe him, but it didn't matter. This was a power play. Anton wasn't afraid for himself, he wanted to have dirt on someone else. Maybe Pastore, too. I didn't care about his problems. I stifled a yawn.

Anton glanced at the rearview again and frowned. "You said before something of a van. I think that –" There was a *pop*, and the back window shattered; the dash and steering wheel were misted with blood. Anton slumped forward onto the wheel. I ducked, and pushed down on the gas pedal with my left hand and did my best to steer with my right. Two more silenced rounds came through the opening in my direction, punching holes in the windshield. I sideswiped a parked car and kept going. I didn't bother to look back. I knew who it was, and driving this way was difficult enough. I could barely see over the dashboard.

I swung a left onto Ridge Avenue against the light. A car swerved, missing me, and skidded on the wet roadway, running headlong through the side of the Dunkin' Donuts on the corner. I stole a look; the red van steered around the mess and followed. It was no good here – the Volvo was faster than the van but there was too much traffic on the big street for me to get by. He would catch up too easily. I spun a right onto a narrow, one lane, one-way street between a hairdresser's and a shuttered grocery store and went left again, fishtailing, the rear tire hitting the curb, halting me, and I snapped three shots at the van's windshield through the driver's side window, but Anton's body fell against me, spoiling my aim. I did my best to push him away and drive. My hands were sticky with his blood.

The guy was shooting at me out his side window; he was either left-handed or he practiced a lot. These roads were difficult to drive anyway – they were in poor condition, and wet, they were worse, but it spoiled his aim. He tried for me again as I spun a right turn. His shot blew out the picture window of the corner row house. I went left and clipped the front end of a car as its driver breeched the intersection. I kept going, but I could smell anti-freeze; the radiator was damaged. The engine wouldn't last long. I held down the gas pedal and drove three blocks more, slipping down a street paved in brick, the Volvo easily out-distancing the van. The next corner had a No Outlet sign posted. Steam pushed out of the front end. The wipers couldn't keep up with the rain. Fifty feet ahead was a chest-high stone wall, open to a walkway on its far right side. The van was a block behind. On foot, they'd have me; I needed to make some noise. I floored the accelerator, and spun the wheel hard to the left as I braced myself against the dashboard. I crashed into the last home's porch front, demolishing the brick footer in its far corner. Anton's body slammed into the steering wheel, setting the horn blaring. The porch roof caved in and fell across the hood. I looked up; the van was coming on. I shoved Anton's body out of the way and braced the back of my forearm against the steering wheel, drew a bead on the driver and pulled the trigger four times. Three rounds punched through the van's windshield on the driver's side; the fourth pull resulted in a *click.* I kicked open the passenger door and ran through the downpour, staying low, keeping the car between the shooter and me, and vaulted the wall as he snapped off a shot; the bullet whined past my ear.

On the other side the ground fell away dramatically; I landed hard and slid partway down a rocky but wooded hillside before I ran into an outcropping that stopped my progress. Pain roared up my left side. I struggled to my feet and looked around through the knee-high weeds and brush. Near me, a terraced steel and concrete staircase led from the roadway above to a narrow cross street a hundred and fifty feet below, fronted by a row of houses on its far side. Beyond that were more blocks of row houses, all leading down to the railroad, the Schuylkill River, and across that, the distant lights of suburban Belmont Hills. A steeple breached the horizon.

I heard the van doors open and slam shut and the engine race as its tires spun out on the wet roadway, the van backing out of the dead end, probably to double back and try to beat me to the bottom of the hill, while one of them gave chase on foot.

I moved farther away from the stairway and the lights, across the slope, slipping, holding onto the trees where I could. I had to take care; to turn an ankle now would be fatal. The rain made the slope even more treacherous, but at least the noise covered any sounds I was making. This wooded hillside was broad. I couldn't see to its end. Forty feet in, I ducked and took cover in a rocky depression. The ground here was wet with rain. I was soaked. I held the empty pistol by the barrel and watched as a man's silhouette broached the wall and raced down the staircase in pursuit. This was the shooter. He was holding the pistol in his left hand. In the dark, I couldn't make out his features, but could see that he was tall and athletic; he vaulted the rail and checked the spaces under the staircase, and scanned the hillside. He kept low. I stopped breathing. I had a chance as long as he believed that I was still armed. Rainwater dripped off my chin.

Above us, an old man's voice sounded. "I see you, you son of a bitch. Get back up here." He'd bellied up to the wall, and was looking down at the guy with the gun. He was holding a folded newspaper over his head to protect him from the shower. Streetlight glinted off his spectacles. He'd either not heard the gunshots or mistook them for thunder. He yelled again, "Yeah, you. Don't think I don't see you. The cops are on the way."

I hoped he was telling the truth. I don't like cops, but I needed them now. The shooter ignored him, searching the slope, crouched, wary – hunting for me.

Below us, on the street, the van pulled up and slowed to a stop. Sirens sounded in the distance. The shooter stood there a few moments more, listening, and pulled himself back up onto the stairs and started down.

The old guy up by the wall hollered, "That's okay, your buddy here's too drunk to run, asshole. You won't get far." He hadn't realized Anton was dead.

The shooter met the van on the street below. I had a bad moment, wondering if they would decide to come up the hill after me, but after about five seconds of discussion, the guy driving moved over to the passenger seat and the shooter got in behind the wheel. They drove away, slowly. I closed my eyes for a second and realized that I was exhausted.

I heard a car slow to a stop above me, and the old guy began to yell, "This prick ran his car into my porch. Another one took off down the stairs."

I had to move. The guys in the van knew that I was nearby, on foot, and would have to move toward them, away from the police. I made my way down the slope, carefully, stopping behind a tree as the cop up on the wall swept the hillside with his flashlight beam. He gave that up and went back to the wreck. I considered using the stairs, but that would leave me in a bad spot if the guys in the van doubled back. At the bottom I checked the street from cover before I took a chance and revealed myself. The streets here were empty. The rain was tapering off to a steady shower. I crossed and headed downhill toward Main Street and the Friday night crowds. I felt dead tired.

15

This neighborhood was called Manayunk, a Lenape word that roughly translates as "Place to drink." Even though I was soaked to the skin, my throat was dry.

I moved in a series of dashes, from one protected spot – a doorway, the mouth of an alley – to another. I was thirty feet from a corner when headlights lit the roadway behind me, and an engine revved hard. I kicked in a rotting gate to a narrow passageway – a ginnel – between two row homes and dove over the trashcans that blocked the way through to the backyards. Out on the street, I heard the van skid to a stop. Its doors opened and closed and it sped up again. I guessed that the driver and passenger were doing their little dance again. I hopped two fences. A motion-activated security light came on in the second back yard. I considered hiding in the breezeway of a darkened home, behind a propane grill covered in gray plastic, but gave that up and clambered up on top of the grill, climbed to the shed roof, shinnied up a run of soil pipe and crawled over the back edge of the main roof.

I lay there in two inches of rainwater, gasping from the effort and peered over the edge. The shooter came through the alley, moving cautiously. I cursed my lack of ammunition; he'd be an easy shot. He moved through the block's backyards slowly.

I found myself blinking, and shook my head. I was really feeling the effort, and had to fight the urge to close my eyes and lie there. I crawled away from the edge and stood, walking out to look over the front, but I felt dizzy, and went down on all fours the rest of the way. The street was empty. Creeping back, I watched the shooter exit the other end of the alley.

I waited a little longer than a reasonable interval, and went back to look over the front edge again. I was in time to see him get back into the van at the end of the block, in the passenger seat this time. They drove another block and took a left. I looked down at myself; I was a mess – wet, dirty, disheveled.

I climbed back down to the shed roof. The back storm window was down. I took out my knife and pried at the bottom edge, bowing it past the point the window would slip off its track. I pushed it up, out of the way and tried the sash behind it. It was unlocked but tight. I had to fight it open. I felt weak as a kitten. The window opened to the back bedroom. I listened for anything – any sound of an occupant that I may have missed. There was nothing. I climbed inside, lowered the sash, and went to the door, leaving wet footprints on the carpet.

As I opened the door to the hallway, there was a *thump* on the floor below, and something charged up the stairs. In the dark, I couldn't see what it was through the railing, just a suggestion of an outline. It turned toward me at the top of the stairs – a huge dog. I slammed the door closed. The dog hurtled into it, shaking its frame, and began to bark.

My eyes adjusted to the darkness. This was a child's room, a girl's. There was a white vanity and mirror, and lots of oversized, stuffed animals. Crayon drawings were stuck to the walls with cellophane tape.

The dog kept up its racket, and scratched at the door with both paws, trying to claw his way through. Opposite the door to the hallway was a closed door to the middle room. I unlatched the door to the adjoining room as quietly as I could and threw a shoe into the middle room. The dog went for it. As I heard it race around to get at me, I went out into the hallway, shut the rear doorway and got the middle room door closed before the dog knew what happened. It kept up the barking and scratching.

My head ached. I gulped down some water from the bathroom sink and threw some on my face, and felt a little better. I did a cursory search of the home to see if these people had a gun, or keys to a car that I could use. Nothing. The crucifix on the wall over the bed was all I needed to know that looking for jewelry would be a waste of time. Catholic ladies owned one piece that never came off their finger. I looked in the closet. There was nothing there for me. The man of the house must have been a tank. All of his shirts would have wrapped around me twice. The dog kept it up. I considered calling for a cab to pick me up there, but I couldn't know how long it might take or when the family would be coming home. The neighbors might hear the dog and call the police.

Outside, I made my way deeper into the neighborhood. I was on Baker Street, fifty feet shy of Green Street, when between houses I caught a glimpse of a train headed to Center City on the trestle over Cresson Street. I decided to run for it. Half a block in, I heard an engine race. The red van came hurtling down the hill toward me, about a hundred feet away. I took off, crossed Green, staying on Baker, running against the flow of traffic and turned down Carson Street, slipping a little on the cobblestones, and dashed under the trestle toward the station entrance. I bolted up the stairs, gasping as I got to the top. The train was pulling away from the station, but hadn't yet picked up speed. I ran the length the platform. It felt like I was running through Jell-O, but I was gaining on the train and I jumped down to the rail bed and raced, catching up to the locomotive. I got a hand on its back step and grabbed onto the lowest of the three safety chains that were hammocked across its back door, and hauled myself up, straining, getting a foot on a fat hydraulic line under the step. I swung myself up sitting across the back step and held on.

I was in time to see the shooter kneeling between the rails to take aim, drawing a bead on me, even as the train rushed away from him. It was a long moment before he pointed the muzzle skyward and stood. I was out of range; it would be a wasted shot. Him knowing that bothered me more than if he had blasted away at me. He turned and made for the stairs. The train took a curve in the track and he disappeared from view.

I struggled to catch my breath as I rode the back step of the train past the upper floors of houses abutting the tracks. Why did they kill Anton? Why were they after me? Two minutes later we stopped at Wissahickon Station. I felt exhausted and could barely hold my eyes open, but looked at the street going past the parking lot. If those guys caught up to the train I was done. I willed the train to move. It did, finally, and as we picked up speed the ground of the neighborhood came up to track level. The engineer sounded the horn as we approached a crossing – two long, one short, one long – and we passed the road, barricades down, lights flashing. On either side of the tracks here, vegetation – junk trees, kudzu – had overwhelmed the right-of-way. There was another crossing, and we stopped for the next station, East Falls. Cresson Street paralleled the tracks here; there were cars parked diagonally, nosed toward the tracks. Across the narrow street were homes showing signs of age.

We took more time at this stop, taking on and discharging passengers. As we pulled away, I saw the van roaring down a cross street. It made the turn onto Cresson as we came up to speed, about two hundred feet ahead of it. They were able to shorten the distance from the train before the ground rose up on both sides while the tracks ran at grade. The streets were out of view through the brush. As we traveled, the ground rose and fell intermittently; at times we soared over the rooftops, others, we ran though a deep crevasse of vines and weeds.

We stopped at Allegheny to take on some passengers, but when we pulled away a transit cop on the platform saw me and yelled, and spoke into his radio.

As we picked up speed again, I scanned the streets we crossed where I could. The neighborhoods were getting rougher; burnt-out factory buildings mingled with rows of run-down homes. The grade rose and fell some more, the tracks here cut a bold diagonal swath, the right-of-way bisecting the grid of streets. I shook my head, and tried to keep my bearings but it was difficult; the frame of reference from the back of the train was foreign to me. As we rode a trestle across a southbound street, I saw the van, a block and a half behind, running a traffic light to try to keep up with the train.

We slowed, rolling under the bridge that carried Broad Street over the tracks. I jumped off the back of the train as we came into the next station, North Broad. I ran down the rail bed between the tracks, back the way we'd come, two, three hundred feet, and when just shy of Broad, I clambered up the wet grass of the embankment to the street level. Twelve-foot storm fencing separated railroad property from the sidewalk. I followed it, pushing my way between the fence and bramble until I found a gap in the chain-link and stepped through. The buildings across the street all appeared to be vacant, save a dialysis center. I was disoriented, and took a few moments to right myself. I felt sick and could barely keep moving. Then I saw what I'd been looking for. I dashed across Broad Street to the subway entrance.

I went down the stairs to the mezzanine and showed the cashier Dougherty's badge. She looked up at me and frowned at my appearance, and just nodded and buzzed me in. I made my way down to the track level, holding onto the railing. My legs felt like rubber. There were a few people waiting for the train, some going to work and some going home. Tracks ran on either side of the platform

An old drunk was carrying on a monologue for anyone who would listen. "Trains here used to run all night, every night. That was back when the country was strong. We made things, right here in Philadelphia. SEPTA messed it all up. Bought all them subway cars from Japan, back there in the eighties. Put Budds on their ass. This last batch of trains, they bought from the Ko—reans. Them cars all out of service now." He paused, searching the crowd for an audience, and returned to his main theme, "You know it. Trains ran all night then. All night, every night." He caught me staring. I must have looked to him like a sympathetic listener. He moved toward me and said, "All night long. You could catch a train into Center City from right here at three hours past midnight, you wanted to." He sang, "Three hours past midnight," and laughed, and said, "just like the old song. You probably too young to know that one." He laughed again and said, "You look like you been having a hell of a night." He looked more closely, frowned and pointed at my chest and said, "Hey, you all right?"

I looked down; there were bloodstains on Marcolina's shirt. I pointed vaguely at my scalp and said, "Yeah, thanks. I hit my head. It bled a lot. I think I'm okay."

"You need to be careful. You should get yourself looked at."

I nodded, and heard a train in the tunnel, and moved down the platform. Something was wrong. I wasn't doing well. The drunk followed me and said, "This here's the last local. Only other train's an express. Nothing else running on these tracks till five in the morning. I been riding these trains all my life. You know it."

I thought about the seltzer water Brenda had insisted on getting for me at the party. It was probably too late to do any good, but I stuck two fingers down my throat and vomited in the corner. The drunk said, "That's right. If it don't agree with you, you got to get it up." I retched again, and spit, to clear my mouth. My head ached.

I heard the metal-on-metal squeal of the train pulling into the station, and wiped at the strands hanging from my lip. The drunk said, "Come on, young fellow, you don't want to miss your train." He helped me on board. The other riders avoided us. I moved to a seat that afforded me a view of the platform. My eyes were watering. I wiped them with my handkerchief.

As the doors closed, I heard someone calling out. We pulled away as the shooter came down the stairs at a run. I ducked, but he saw me anyway.

The drunk was oblivious to it all, and said, "That's too bad. That fellow missed his train." He pointed to the far side of the platform. "He'll have to get the express, if it does him any good."

We were picking up speed and rushed out of the station into the tunnel. I struggled to think; my head was throbbing. "What stations does the express train stop at?"

"Next stops they make are Girard, then Fairmount and City Hall. It won't do me any good, but if you're stopping at one of them, the express train gets there sooner, most of the time."

I couldn't focus on the lights in the tunnel flying by. They made me feel worse. I squeezed my eyes shut and tried to breathe deeply. We slowed and stopped at Susquehanna-Dauphin. The old drunk said, "This here's as far as I go." I could hear another train coming. He said, "That's the express, now." I nodded. He said, "You sure you going to be all right?" I nodded. "All right, then. You take care." He got off with three other passengers, and four got on. I hesitated a moment and got off just before the doors closed.

16

I wanted to run down what Anton had told me about the smugglers. Out on Broad Street near Susquehanna, I bought some Excedrin and a bottle of water in a shop run by two gay Bengali men who clucked and fretted over my appearance. I swallowed three of the tablets with some water and scanned the street. My phone was gone – I'd lost it somewhere between here and Manayunk. Dougherty's wallet, keys and empty pistol were still there.

One of the Bengalis sold me a burner. I dialed a city number and heard a woman say, "Philadelphia Fire Department, Dispatcher Weaver."

I held a hand against my free ear to hear her over the bad pop music on the store's radio. "Hi. This is Sergeant Dougherty, Sheriff's. There was a medic unit dispatched to an auto accident on Delaware Avenue early last night. I need to know what hospital any of the patients went to."

"Hold on please." I waited about thirty seconds and she came back on the line, "One patient, an adult white male, was transported to Jefferson. The others at the scene refused service. Is there anything else you need, Sergeant?"

"No. Thank you."

I hung up and made another call. A tired voice said, "Night Command, Captain Miller." He sounded as though permanently aggrieved. Night Command was a trash assignment.

"I need to speak to Armand Ruggieri. He works last out in the Sixth."

"Who's calling?"

"Nobody. I just need to get in touch with him."

"That ain't gonna flush. I need a name."

"Ok. Tell him this is Sergeant Joe Dougherty, Sheriff's."

I imagined his lips moving as he wrote and he said, "All right. Give me a number you can be reached at."

I read him the number and hung up. I drank some more water and felt a little better, and looked out at the street. One of the proprietors bothered me about loitering. I gave him one of Dougherty's twenties and told him to leave me alone. Now that I was able to stand in one spot, the night caught up with me. Everything hurt. I rotated my shoulder in both directions; it was really sore, but I hadn't re-broken the collarbone or done any serious damage. I felt like I could sleep around the clock.

I thought again about giving this up. I could go back to Dougherty's house, toss it for whatever money he had and then go home. He probably had enough hidden there for me to replace the Camry.

Then I thought about George again, and knew that I had to keep going. Letting this go unanswered would do me a lot of damage. Nobody would be likely to blame me for George getting killed, but professionals might not feel like working with me anymore. Guys in the life would expect you to do something.

The caffeine in the Excedrin would start to help a little, but I'd have to be careful. I thought some more about the guys in the van – the smart thing for them to do would be to go to ground, but they kept coming on, determined to kill me. Nothing about the whole night had felt smart. It felt rushed, panicked – too much left to chance.

My phone rang a few minutes later. I answered, "Yeah."

There was a pause. "Who is this?"

I said, "You've done business with me before and it's always worked out well. For both of us."

Armand was quiet long enough for me to know that he knew who he was speaking with. I continued, "I need a ride. Come and double park somewhere on Broad between Dauphin and Susky. I'll see you and we can talk. Okay?"

"All right. Fifteen minutes." He hung up.

The music on the radio ended and the announcer said, "The rain clouds are gone, and there's going to be clear skies and hot weather this morning. Police marine units have recovered still another body from the Delaware River tonight. That brings the total to three in the last twenty-four hours. In South Philadelphia, Fire Department personnel rescued a man from the trunk of his car. Patrons of a parking garage heard sounds coming from the vehicle and alerted authorities —"

I needed a car. I counted the money I'd taken from Brenda's apartment. There were eighteen hundred and thirty-five dollars. I'd have to make that work. I found the napkin that Tom had given me. It was soaked, but the number was still legible. A man answered the phone, "Best."

"I'm looking for Flipper."

"That's me. What can I do for you?"

"The guy at the Idle Hour said you could sell me something that moves."

He was quiet for a moment and said, "Look here - things are real funny right now. No offense, but I'm gonna have to call the guy first."

"Fair enough."

"Y'all got a number I can reach you at?"

"I'll call back. Half an hour?"

"That'll work." He hung up.

17

Armand was driving a late-model silver Buick Regal. I got in and said, "Nice short."

He didn't comment on my appearance, just nodded and said, "Yeah, I like it." He put the car in gear and we headed south on Broad Street. "I'm not sure how the original owner lost it, but my guess is he got caught doing something he shouldn't have."

"Were you in on the Pastore bust?"

Armand said, "That's you – right to it."

"I'm sorry. How are you, Armand? How are things in the Sixth?" I rolled down my window,

"I'm good. The Sixth, I don't know. I'm doing something else now. No. I wasn't part of the bust. I'd have liked to. Man, I'd have liked to. I didn't get invited."

"What's his status now?"

Armand gave me a look and said, "You want to know something particular, you should ask."

"Just whatever you might know about him."

"The main thing I know is that he and his buddy the mayor fucked me and everybody else when we got hired. We qualified for food stamps, our starting pay was so bad."

"Yeah, I heard."

"A reporter asked him about that. He said, 'Nobody forced them to take the job.'"

"Sounds like a real sweetheart."

"So what else you need to know? He's crooked as the day is long, but up until now he's been untouchable."

"Why? Connections?"

Armand thought while we traversed three or four blocks given over to Temple University property. He said, "Mostly connections." He stopped for a light. "My own guess is that everybody's afraid of him."

"Why's that?"

"I think that he's got dirt on everybody he's ever done business with. The Feds plan to go inside his house this morning, and a lot of people are unhappy about that. Even some of the guys executing the warrant."

"But you never had anything to do with him?"

"No. The only time I ever see him is at the communion breakfast – League of The Sacred Heart."

"I never took you for a believer."

"I'm not." The light changed and we moved with traffic. "I'm a union trustee."

"Congratulations. Since when?"

"Since the last three elections, but thanks. We do shit like that, the breakfast and whatnot. Politics. Anyway, Pastore is always there, taking communion, genuflecting deeply, acting all fucking pious. Last year he's posing with the cardinal in the vestibule, thanking him for the beautiful sermon, and thirty seconds later he corners D'Allesandro on the steps outside and calls the good justice a cocksucker for ruling against him in some court case. Comical."

"So Pastore's just playing the game, too?"

"I don't think so. I think a lot of guys born lucky are true believers. They prefer to think their good fortune is all part of God's plan." We passed by the Liacouras Center on our right. A banner hung from the marquee, reading, "Home of The Owls!" Armand said, "Did you watch any of the finals?"

"Go Wildcats. Yeah, a lot. I was laid up."

"Why?"

"I had an accident. It's a long story. Did you see the Temple – Iowa game?"

"No."

"Too bad. There was this kid who played for Iowa who reminded me of you – skinny guy – cheap shot artist. Spent the whole game hacking at guys wrists. He fouled out."

Armand chuckled. "How's Susan?"

"She's fine."

"Good looking woman. Tell her I said hello."

I said, "This judge – D'Allesandro – what's his story?" We stopped at a traffic light.

"Her story. Donna D'Allesandro. Common pleas judge. Also a neighborhood girl. She's connected politically – came up fast. She's about forty. Not bad looking, but kind of twisted."

"Twisted how?"

"You're on the stand, she'll ask you a direct question and when you turn to answer her, she'll flash you. She doesn't wear panties under the robe, and she's an old-fashioned girl. Big muff." Armand held his hands a foot apart. "Doesn't matter if she's done it to you before – fucks you up, every time."

"What's her connection to Pastore?"

"They're sort of chummy, most of the time. They might have been a thing for a while. I don't know." He shrugged. "The neighborhood means a lot to both of them." The light changed and we pulled into traffic.

"What about Eddie Reilly?"

"He's in the wind."

"Who brings drugs into Philadelphia?"

"That's abrupt." He looked at me and back to the road. "Lots of people."

"Can you expand on that a little?"

"No, my shift ends at eight and then I'm going home. I still wouldn't be finished telling you about the Philadelphia drug trade. Again, maybe if you were more specific about what you wanted, I could be more helpful."

"Okay, there's no need for sarcasm."

"I apologize."

"You ever hear of Eric Anton?"

"No. Who's that?"

"He was a gangster. Slovak."

"I never heard of him, but that doesn't mean anything. He could just be somebody that I haven't heard of. A lot of those guys make a big splash, but most don't last. You said 'was.' Dead?"

"Yeah."

"You?"

"No."

Armand seemed unconvinced. I said, "Really, no. Not my thing. But to my point, he seemed to be somebody. It seemed like he had an organization."

"Could be, but I never ran into him."

"Is there anyone new? Is there more of anything around lately?"

"Define 'lately.'"

"A few months."

He shot me a look.

I said, "I'm not sure." I thought about the log entries on Pastore's boat; they'd ended before December. "No earlier than New Year's."

Armand thought for a moment and said, "There are always new players in the game, but no, there's been no significant increase in quantity or quality."

I hesitated a moment and said, "Did anything happen last night?"

"What do you mean?"

"I'm not sure. Anything unusual?"

"Nothing that has anything to do with me."

I thought about it for a few blocks. Armand broke in and said, "Are you talking about anything that I need to be aware of?"

"No, I'm just trying to track something down. Why, are you back in Narcotics?"

"No, thank god. I'm dealing with a higher class clientele, lately." His phone rang. He said, "Excuse me," and answered, and said to the caller, "Good, gimme ten minutes," and hung up. He said to me, "This thing you're trying to track down – would it have anything to do with George Rafferty?"

I took my time and said, "Yes, and the same bunch are out for me. George was my partner."

Armand nodded. "I don't have to tell you about what happens to cop-killers."

"George wasn't a cop anymore."

"Retired is close enough for some of us."

I nodded. "I'm trying to take care of it."

"I hope you do."

I took that at face value. Armand would do whatever he chose to. We were coming up to the Blue Horizon. The darkened venue looked forlorn; I noticed a few slates missing from its mansard. I said, "Do you still train?"

"Yeah. Not like I used to, but yeah. I like to stay in shape." Armand glanced at the old arena as we cruised past it. "I've got to find a new gym. The place I'm at now, too many guys there are guys I've locked up." He glanced my way and said, "I ran into your old friend Jimmy Florio a couple weeks ago."

"I don't know who that is."

Armand chuckled. "That's okay. He was acting squirrelly. I asked him what was new. Jimmy never won a dime playing cards. Spent two minutes telling me that nothing was happening. I figured he had something going on, but he beat it before I could really talk to him."

I nodded and said, "Still follow the local fights?"

"As much as there is a local scene, yes. There's some good bouts in that hall up by the Northeast Airport."

"Do I have enough drag with you to ask a favor?"

Armand made a gesture that took in the interior of the car. "What do you call this?"

"'This' is a ride. I need a favor."

"Try me."

"There are a couple of guys who are probably being held at the Fourteenth right now. Can you get them sent to the roundhouse?"

"What are they being held for?"

"I'm not sure. They got picked up on Tulpehocken Street in Germantown."

"I know where Tulpehocken Street is. Did these guys kill George?"

"No. They aren't responsible for that."

"This is a lot. I'll have to take care of another guy, maybe two. You sure you want this?"

"Yeah."

He took out his cell and thumbed up a call, and said, "Hey, this is Armand. You holding a couple guys from a job on Tulpehocken Street?" He listened and said to me, "Big guys, tatted up?" I nodded and Armand said into the phone, "Yeah, that's them. Can you put them in a wagon to headquarters?" He listened and said to me, "They got a lawyer on the way." He said into the phone, "He's an asshole. Can you tell him you sent them over to Northwest Detectives?" There was a pause and he said "Thanks," and hung up. "Those two are being held on disorderly conduct. They'd probably be cut loose anyway, but they called this lawyer, Brian Lawlor. Real two-hander.

Penn Charter boy. I'll call a guy at Northwest and have him tell Lawlor they sent those guys somewhere else."

"Thanks, Armand."

We drove past the Metropolitan. The peeling whitewash on the old theater's façade put me in mind of psoriasis. Armand said, "You wanna tell me what I did all that for?"

"I need to talk to those guys, and then I'd like them out of my way for the rest of the night."

"Their lawyer will find them eventually. They'll get out in a few hours."

"That's all right. I'll take a few hours." I added, "I'll make sure to share anything that might help you."

"You're gonna share more than that." He rapped his knuckles on the dashboard, twice.

I got the message. His help would cost me two times his usual fee. I'd thought he would hold me up for more. I answered his raps with two of my own, and said, "Sure."

"How are you gonna talk to them at headquarters?"

"I'll think of something."

"You always were a wooly guy." We stopped for the light at Fairmount Avenue. "Figure on them getting there in an hour or so. You'll probably have an hour, maybe a two-hour window after that to talk things over with them before their lawyer gets there."

"Thanks."

Across the street was the long-vacant Divine Loraine Hotel. Scaffolding covered its front and sides. Banners that hung across its front proclaimed, "Live In a Landmark!" and "Now Leasing!"

Armand looked at the building and said, "That's long overdue."

I agreed. "About thirty years."

We moved as the light changed. I was still tired, but I could feel the caffeine from the Excedrin beginning to work.

Armand drove another few blocks and said, "There anything else I can do for you, anything you want to know?"

"No."

"Then there's something I want to know. What are you doing working in town? I thought we had an agreement."

I'd been waiting for this. "We do, Armand. This is a one-off."

"No more after this." He pulled over at Race Street. City Hall loomed, straight ahead.

"No. You got it." I looked around the intersection, I needed to go out to University City, but Armand didn't need to know exactly where. I said, "Can you take me to 30th Street Station?"

"Sorry. I got somewhere else I need to be," he looked at his dashboard clock, "in a few minutes."

"There is one other thing – do you have any ammo? Nine millimeter?"

"No. I pack a forty."

"You got a spare piece?"

"I'm not that kind of cop."

I said, "Thanks, Armand," and got out of the Regal. He flipped on his flashers, pulled a u-turn in the big street and drove north.

18

The rain hadn't done anything to cool the temperature – it felt even muggier. I got off the trolley in the underground station, walked north and was sweating as I knocked on the door of a white stucco, three-story single just past Race. There were no homes on the other side of the street. The ground sharply sloped away to the rail yard past eight-foot chain link fencing and beyond that, the expressway and the Schuylkill River, and past its far bank, the park.

I knocked again and Harry opened the door a crack and looked out. "Oh. It's you." He was wearing a blue terry-cloth bathrobe. He stuck his head out the door and looked up and down the street. He looked back at me and said, "You don't look good."

"Are you going to let me in?"

He stared at me for a moment more and opened the door wider, still standing half- concealed by it. "I suppose so."

I went inside, stepping past him and into the living room. He closed the door. I said, "You don't seem glad to see me."

"I'm surprised to see you. I can't say that I'm glad. It wasn't a good idea for you to come here." He kept his right hand out of sight behind him. "You should call first."

He meant, call first, and then don't come. "I need help." He stared at me. I continued, "I'm not here to make trouble for you. Put away the cannon."

He stared another second and said, "Whatever it is that you're into, you should forget it," he put the little pistol away in the drawer of a living room hutch. He seemed relieved to get it out of his hand; Harry had an aversion to firearms. "I heard on the radio tonight that there was trouble earlier this evening. That you?"

There was no reason to lie to Harry. He'd believe what he wanted to. "Yeah."

"A dead cop? And you come here, to my home?"

"That wasn't me."

"No, but it's all part of whatever you're wrapped up in, isn't it?" I nodded and he said, "That's disappointing." He moved to a hallway closet. "You'll get a bad reputation that way." He took out a light blue golf shirt on a hanger. "You wouldn't like prison. Believe me."

"Nobody's going to prison."

"Hah. That's what I thought. Two and a half years in The Don taught me different. Stone walls and iron bars, just like in the movies. It's no joke." Inwardly I cringed; I'd heard Harry's prison story before. He gestured toward the powder room and said, "Get yourself cleaned up and put this on. You can't go around looking like that." He handed me the shirt.

"Thanks."

He looked down at my trousers. "My pants wouldn't fit you."

"That's okay." I took the shirt by the hanger. University of Pennsylvania was embroidered above the pocket. "Helping somebody with their homework?"

He gave me a dirty look. "I'm not in the mood for comedy."

I went into the little bathroom, stripped off Marcolina's shirt, and looked at my reflection. I looked like I felt. There was a softball-sized mark on my left side – beginning to bruise – probably from when I'd landed and slid down the hill in Manayunk. I probed it with my right hand. I didn't think I'd broken a rib, but it hurt a lot. I fingered my collarbone, too, and rotated my shoulder again. It hurt, but was probably okay. The bandage on my right shoulder seemed clean enough. I washed the remains of Anton's blood off my face and arms, dried myself with paper towels, and put on the golf shirt. I came out with Marcolina's ruined sports shirt in my hand. "What should I do with this?"

"Out here." Harry walked us into the kitchen. I dropped the shirt into his waste can.

He continued with his story. "If they had let me out after the first night, I'd have lived the life of a saint for the rest of my days on earth. I was scared shitless." He ran a hand over his scalp; his gray hair was so light, and cut so short that his head appeared to be shaved. "You want something to drink?"

"Yeah, water, please."

He filled a pint glass from the tap for me. I took a big swallow. It tasted good. I was still shaky. I drank off half the glass and said, "Thanks."

He waved it away and continued, "My second day inside, this big Mohawk thought I looked like an easy win. I broke his cheekbone in four places — he almost lost an eye. After that it wasn't too bad. I made a few friends. We watched each other's backs. Sit." He pulled out a chair for me at the kitchen table, and he sat down.

"The worst of it was, after about two months inside, I'm walking down the hallway from chow and I realize I'm at home. I'd gotten comfortable with being in prison." He shook his head. "The things you can get used to. When they let me out, the Canadian government requested that I leave the country. Fortunately for me, that was after the peanut farmer granted amnesty to all us dissenters."

"What's your point?"

"My point is that I did my time like a man. I went in alone and I came out the same way. I'm not going inside again. Now what do you need?"

"Mostly information. Is anybody moving stones?"

"What, hot stuff?"

"No, at least not hot here. I mean anything coming into Philadelphia without going through customs. Anything smuggled."

"You know that this is happening?"

"No, I'm just asking."

"I haven't heard about anything like that. It's not the kind of thing that a guy my size would likely be approached to handle, but I haven't heard about anything. Would this be a one-time thing?"

"No, this would have been an ongoing operation."

"Then, no, nothing like that is happening. If it was once in a while, maybe yes, but what you say, no."

"What about the Asians? Don't they like different stuff? Stuff you wouldn't deal with?"

"No. That's the gold. They like twenty-two, twenty-four carat stuff. Higher content alloys. Those are softer, more difficult to work with, but that's what they like. The stones – no. Stones are stones."

"Nobody's moving gold, either?"

"Not that I've heard."

I mulled this over and said, "What do you know about Vic Pastore?"

"He's bringing in stones? I thought he got locked up?"

"He is locked up. No, I mean in general, what do you know about him?"

"He's a cock-sucker, that's what I know about him."

"How so?"

"He had his bitch girlfriend D'Allesandro rule against me – invoke eminent domain statutes to fuck me out of a property I had over on Second Street, just south of Girard, there, where his friends built that apartment complex and mall. I took a bath."

"Were you holding them up?"

"No way, I wanted to sell. This was an investment property, nothing else. Pricks never made me a realistic offer. Am I allowed to ask why you're asking me all this?"

I needed help. I said, "Somebody has been using a boat to meet ships out in the Delaware Bay and offload goods. I'd like to know what those goods are."

"How big is the boat?"

"Big enough. Fifty-footer."

"So this would be Pastore's boat, then?" He waited for me, and said, "That's all right. You'd rather not say. Okay. Somebody's fifty-foot boat – that's big enough to be making a significant contribution. And it would have to. The overhead to run something like that would be a killer."

"That might not be a consideration."

"The other thing to consider then is that it would be conspicuous. Whoever was using it would want to be bringing in something big, otherwise, why not use something smaller? Why not just fly? There was an old-timer I knew, big fellow, used to move a hundred pounds of gold every week, as long as the prices were right. He flew commercial flights."

I humored him. "How did he move it? A carry-on?"

Harry shook his head. "He always carried a very expensive attaché case. It would catch the eye of any new inspector. My friend made sure that it was always full of very dull, very innocent paperwork." Harry grinned and said, "He moved the gold in small plates, sewn into the lining of his suit coat."

"Nice." I'd heard this story before, too.

"That man had style. Taught me a lot." Harry sighed and added, "Been gone a long time, now."

I interrupted his reverie. "With this boat, I think somebody's capitalizing on easy availability."

"Such as the owner not really needing it because he's incarcerated." He smiled, having fun with this, despite himself. "Come on. You know what they're bringing in."

I hadn't until that moment. Whatever I'd been dosed with had clouded my head.

Harry's robe gapped open, revealing a gold Star of David hanging on a thin gold chain amidst a thatch of gray chest hair. I said, "You haven't been asleep tonight."

He frowned, annoyed that I wouldn't play. "What's wrong with you?"

"Don't get defensive. You got company?"

He grimaced at me and said, "Yeah." He stood. "As a matter of fact, I do. So if there's nothing else I can do for you . . ."

I got up and said, "There is. I need some ammo. Nine millimeter."

He shook his head. "Guns are the tools of savages."

"You came to the door with –"

"Yeah, with a gun in my hand. I live in the world, where there are a lot of vicious cocksuckers who know that I sometimes carry about my person precious stones and or large sums of money. I also keep it handy when somebody bangs on my door in the middle of the night."

"Sorry."

"I don't use it to earn my daily bread."

"Ok, Harry. I said I was sorry."

He calmed and said, "I only have cartridges for that pea-shooter," he pointed over his shoulder with his thumb. "That won't do you any good."

I shook my head.

He added, "This time of night, the only guy I know can help you is Ron."

"Ron's unhappy with me. Has been for a while."

"He's not mad at you. You hurt his feelings when you partnered up with Redfern."

"I didn't realize he was such a sensitive soul."

"Most of us are. The sooner you realize that, the better off you'll be." He walked me toward the front door and said, "I'll call him, tell him you're stopping by. Nine millimeter?"

"Yeah."

"Shame about Reds."

"Yeah." I walked outside and said, "Thanks, Harry."

He said, "Next time, call first," and shut the door.

19

I needed a car. I dialed Flipper's number. When he answered, I said, "I called earlier. You got something for me?"

"I expected you to call back sooner."

"I got held up."

He hesitated, waiting for me to continue, and said, "Yeah. Come by. I'm on 29th Street, just north of Thompson. Best Auto Repair."

Inwardly, I cursed. It meant backtracking, and another hairy neighborhood. It's difficult to operate in places where you stand out. I lied, playing for time. "I got a stop to make first."

"Make it soon, hear? I wanna go home."

"Right." I broke the connection.

I cabbed to 29th and Girard and walked north. Best Auto Repair was past the next traffic light, on the opposite side of the street, between Thompson and Master. Other than its sign swaying in the breeze above the big overhead door, there was no movement on the street. I walked past a short row of failing brick and joist houses toward Stiles, a small side street. There was a 24-hour grocery store on the far corner.

Like Flipper had told me earlier, it had been a funny night. I wanted to see what would happen if someone went into the garage. I opened the door to the grocery. A buzzer sounded, and a Korean man seated on a stool behind the counter looked up from a newspaper. His face gave away his story – at first apprehensive, then resigned – his life revolved around this little store, in a place where he was needed but unwelcome. He kept his right hand below the counter.

I took a look around – two rows of shelves and a cooler for beer and soda in the back. The walls and ceiling were painted a dull brown. There were no other customers. I saw the man's reflection in the large convex disc mirror mounted in the far corner. He was watching me, mostly because I was something different, something from beyond the four walls of this small store, beyond this neighborhood.

I stepped up to the counter. There were vestiges of a frame – wood and angle iron – the counter had probably once been separated from the store proper by thick sheets of Plexiglas. Likely, the security panels went up after a robbery, but had made shoplifting easier and were taken down.

I said, "Gimme a pack of Marlboro."

The man reached for them in the rack behind him. "Nine seventy-five."

"Do you make deliveries?"

"What? No." He held onto the cigarettes, confused.

I put a twenty on the counter. "Not far. Just take those cigarettes to the garage up the street."

"Hey – no. I can't leave, I'm all alone – why don't you take?"

This part was tricky. I put another twenty on top of the first. "I'm going the other way. Go on. It'll take you two minutes."

He licked his lips and looked at the bills on the counter. He knew that something wasn't right, but the money was likely more than the store would take in before sunrise.

I said, "Please," and put down a third twenty.

He looked up, clearly pained. He glanced around the store. Finally, the bills on the counter overwhelmed his better judgment and he said, "Okay. Well, okay." He put the money in the register and locked it.

I went outside ahead of him. He locked the front door behind us, watching me, and looked around the intersection, wary, vulnerable. He looked at me again and smiled nervously. This was a citizen; he'd taken the money and to him, refusal now was impossible. He set off up 29th Street. I said, "Hey." He turned around, rattled. "You gotta knock hard. He's doing work in there."

He nodded and walked toward the garage. After a few steps he balked and turned around to look at me again. I waved him on, and I walked around the corner in the direction of 28th Street.

I entered the narrow alley that ran through the length of the block from Stiles to Thompson and trotted north, hurdling some bags of trash and a tire, and turning my shoulders sideways to negotiate a tight spot where an ailanthus tree pushed its way through a crack in the pavement. My heel slipped on a pile of dog shit.

At the other end, I waited just shy of the sidewalk. I'd gotten there in time to watch as the shopkeeper crossed Thompson Street. He was behaving as I'd hoped – looking over his shoulder, hurrying and slowing down – the perfect picture of a nervous man. He walked into the next block and out of my line of sight.

Thompson ran one way, eastbound. I looked up and down the street. The parked cars appeared empty, but one at the 28th Street end of the block was parked bucking traffic, and had its driver-side window rolled down – there was no reflection where glass should be.

I stayed where I was and listened. About ten seconds later I heard the grocer banging on the garage door. I waited. Rusty hinges sounded and a conversation that I couldn't make out.

A moment after that there were sounds from the car at end of the block – faint static and a chirp as someone keyed a microphone and spoke under their breath. The car started and drove past me toward 29th and around the corner. Another car roared straight up 29th Street. A third came down Thompson from 30th Street but stopped short of 29th. Two men jumped out and entered the alley that ran behind the garage.

I came down the street and moved around the corner slowly. The block was clotted with vehicles. Men were entering the garage, and the overhead door was rolling open.

Two men lay prone in the street, their hands cinched behind them. One was the storekeeper, complaining loudly, sounding more frightened than outraged. I assumed that the other was Flipper. I heard him say, "Y'all got no warrant, and no probable cause. There's nothing in my shop that's admissible."

A plainclothes cop said, "Shut up."

"There best not be nothing missing in there. Y'all hear me?"

"Shut up."

At the far end of the block, a late-model silver Buick Regal idled. Beyond that, a police wagon and a heavy-duty panel truck were cruising down the street toward the garage.

I moved across the street past a black nineties model Ford sedan and turned into the alley behind the garage. Both of the cops were young. One of them held his radio to his ear; he held his pistol down along his leg. I said "Yo!" They looked up, startled. I continued, "That car in the middle of the street yours? The Ford?"

They looked at each other and back to me. One, a reedy-looking kid said, "Yeah, that's us."

"I need to bring the Crime Scene truck around front, and you got the street blocked. I know you've been told about that."

The other cop said, "We got told to cover the alley. Where else we supposed to put the car?"

"Hey. You want to give me a bunch of lip, we can go talk to Lieutenant Ruggieri."

"No, you got it. Sorry." He moved to go by me, fishing the car keys out of his pants pocket.

I put my hand on his chest. "Stop. What are you supposed to be doing?"

He looked confused, and said, "Standing by." He held up his radio.

"Then do what you've been told to do. I'll move the car." I held out my hand. He hesitated and I said, "Come on, come on."

He handed me the keys. I walked back out and got into the Ford. It started right up. I put it into gear and drove to the Girard Avenue Bridge and back into West Philadelphia.

20

The Ford ran with a bad knock. I parked around the corner from Ron's club and went through the car – under the seats, in the glove compartment – to see if there was anything in it that I could use, but came up empty, save an open plastic liter bottle of water and old fast-food wrappers. Inside the trunk were a spare tire and a bumper jack. This was a stakeout car – confiscated property used in the commission of a crime. There were no emergency lights and no mounted police radio, and I doubted that there would be any sort of GPS device; the police garage had their hands full just keeping the fleet on the streets and running. There was a good chance that Armand would figure me for borrowing the car but I'd make it up to him.

I'd have liked to find some 9mm ammo – even just a few rounds. I'd needed to patch things up with Ron for a while, and I didn't like the idea of going to see him with my hand out. I left the car parked where it was and walked around the corner.

Two men stood on the sidewalk in front of the bar, smoking, and stopped talking as I went inside. A black couple near the door saw me come in. They seemed to resent it. It was loud, but another man spoke to be heard above the music. "You sure you in the right place?"

I ignored him, and made room for myself near the taps. A few more people gave me their attention. When the woman tending bar walked by, I said, "Excuse me, I need to see Mr. Tolliver."

She was small but built solidly, and she carried it well – more importantly, she knew it. Her eyes were almond-shaped and green; they gave her an unusual look, almost Asian. She looked me over and said, "You a cop?"

I smiled and said, "He'll want to talk to me."

She punched numbers on a phone and spoke into it. "Hey. There's a white man out here, wants to speak to you." More of the crowd turned and stared. When she was finished she smirked and said, "I suppose you know what you're doing."

Ron Tolliver came out of the back and focused on me immediately. When he was close enough to be heard, he said, "It's been a while."

Ron was a tough read. He'd been miffed the last time we'd spoken. He wasn't showing anything now. I said, "Do you have a few minutes for me?"

"Come on." He turned and we walked toward the back. The bartender followed us. Everybody in the place had stared a minute ago, but now, no one looked at me. It was like I had become invisible. I looked back at the man who'd first spoken to me; the animosity that had shown on his face was gone, replaced by something else. He put his drink down and left.

We stepped into a back room. It was small – two tables, and a stairway to the second floor. Two men sat at one of the tables, and they stared at me as I came in.

Ron said to me, "You don't look good."

"I know. I got dosed."

"What with?"

"Not sure. Some kind of down. Gave me a killer headache."

"You don't want a drink, then." He said to the bartender, "Leonetta, make a pot of coffee for my guest. Make it strong, please." She left, and Ron said, "You got to excuse some of these people. You took them by surprise. It's not often a white boy walks in here."

"It takes a lot to make me cry."

"I know that." He sat there, staring at me. I couldn't tell if he was angry, or like Harry had said, just disappointed. Ron continued, "I haven't heard from you for a long time. How come you're here now? When you need something?"

Even with the music, it suddenly seemed very quiet in the little room. I sensed the guys at the other table sitting up a little straighter. I said, "You were annoyed with me the last time I saw you."

"Yeah, I was, but I don't stay that way. You know that I never stay that way."

"You didn't use to. I don't know about now, since you've come up in the world."

"No. I got your back."

"My mistake then. I apologize."

He waved it away. "Water under the bridge." He sat at the empty table with his back to the far corner of the room. "Harry sounded upset."

"Harry's an old woman." I took the seat facing him. "I'm doing my best to salvage a job gone bad. Can you help me?"

Ron nodded to one of the men. The guy took a box of Remington cartridges out of his pocket and passed it to me. I put it in my hip pocket. "Thanks."

Ron said, "You're welcome. I hope you don't need them."

"Me, too."

"What else?"

This was going to be trickier. "Who is bringing illegals into Philadelphia?"

Ron didn't react. One of his guys looked up too fast, but covered it pretty well. Ron said, "The short answer to that is a lot of people. Give me some details."

"Somebody has been using a boat to offload illegals from ships in the Delaware Bay, and bring them into the city somewhere."

"And what's your complaint?"

"They stole my property and tried to kill me." I let him think about that for a moment and added, "Ron, if I'm stepping on your toes, say so. Call off the dogs. I'll go home and forget all this."

"They aren't mine or anybody's that I know about." He thought for a few moments and added, "People still want to come to America, and there's plenty folks here looking for cheap labor. There's a lot of money to be made facilitating things."

I said, "Apparently, something happened last night that has a lot of people upset. Have you heard about anything like that?"

"No, I can't say as I have."

"Do you know Vic Pastore?"

"How does he figure?"

"They've been using his boat."

Ron nodded, and seemed to relax. "I had trouble with the commander over in the Eighteenth District a while ago. My usual phone call couldn't do anything for me at the time – she was wrapped up in that thing with the Parking Authority – she suggested that I call Senator Pastore." Ron pronounced the name with the accent on the first syllable. "He took care of the problem for me. Now and then I show him that I haven't forgotten his kindness."

"How bad does he beat you up?"

"Not too bad. Since then, we've helped each other out with a few things. He likes to stay friendly with the ministers out this way, cause he needs to be. He also owns some properties near here."

"What can you tell me about Pastore's troubles that I can't get from the papers?"

"I know that the government isn't through squeezing him. I'm not sure what you're looking for."

"Who does he owe? Who is he afraid of?"

"Nobody and everybody. Vic is the quintessential Philadelphia politician – he's the master of selling you what you already own, mostly by selling himself. Just like his daddy. But you don't get to where he is without selling yourself over and over. That breeds conflict. A man like Pastore is going to run out of people that trust him, and people that he can trust."

"Who does he trust?"

"His man Eddie Reilly. They've known each other since grade school."

"Reilly's disappeared."

"He won't be far. Reilly's a stooge."

"I thought he was a smart guy."

"He's a very smart guy. He realized his limitations a long time ago, and he hitched his wagon to Pastore's star, but he doesn't have the imagination it takes to live a different life than the one he's living. You find him, he'll tell you what you need to know. Excuse me a moment." He took a phone from his pocket and turned away to speak into it. I knew better than to try to listen in. It would have been hopeless anyway; the music seemed to get louder. My head throbbed.

I tried to think it through. If Reilly was still in town, he wouldn't be anywhere like a hotel or motor lodge, where he would have to show a credit card. He would have to be somewhere else, maybe a house or apartment.

Ron finished his call and smiled at me. As though he knew my thoughts, he said, "You'll want to be looking at places that Pastore owns that aren't occupied, or either, at least not listed that way – vacants, or recently vacated." I just nodded.

He continued, "I don't see why you're still messing with scores. Come in with me. You say the word – I'll put you on my crew tomorrow."

"Oh, yeah?" I turned to look at the pair and back. "How would that work out?"

"Everybody in this bar just saw me walk you back here. They already thinking you must be King Kong or Godzilla." He chuckled. "I'm an equal opportunity employer – even got a Cambodian boy working for me now. Think about it. We'd be together again." He got more serious and said, "You shouldn't be working so hard anymore."

We'd had this conversation the last time we'd spoken. The mobs are pyramid organizations – broad, flat pyramids, with a lot of people on the bottom, one guy on top, and very few in between. Not working hard anymore – that was a joke. If I took Ron's offer, I'd be working all the time – worrying about who's coming up, who wanted to take my place. Guys like Ron and Danny Raco spent their lives looking over their shoulders. Ron just hadn't been there long enough to be weary of it yet. I said, "Thanks, but you know me. I like doing my little jobs and then fucking off for the next few months."

Ron nodded. "I could throw you some work, anyway. I know a dude, owns a block of vacants over in The Bottom that he doesn't want to pay taxes on anymore." Ron sniffed the air. "I think he smells smoke."

"I've been trying to avoid working in the hometown."

"Always a good policy, and yet, here you are."

"Here I am."

The bartender set a pot of coffee and two cups on the table. She caught my eye and said, "Y'all need some sugar?"

Ron said, "Leave the man alone, Leonetta."

She gave him a look and walked away.

"I think she likes you," he said, while he poured coffee for us. "You should speak to her before you leave."

"I have all the trouble I need." I tried the coffee. It was too hot to drink.

Ron shook his head. "She's good. She and her girlfriend just came up with a new dodge. They dress up like Jehovah's Witnesses on Sunday mornings and go door to door. Pick out a nice neighborhood. Somebody opens up to tell them go away, Leonetta shows them the gun. They tie them up and go through the house."

"They won't be able to play that out for long."

"They fly the friendly skies. Different towns, different cities. They could play it out indefinitely." He smiled. "You and her could do some good work together."

"I admire her style, but I try to stay away from women with guns."

"I heard you got hurt."

The segue threw me. "Who told you that?"

"It doesn't matter. What matters is that I heard it."

I nodded.

Ron continued, "What do I always say? If you want someone to believe your story, they have to tell it to themselves. That's why the job up in Union City went down so easy. That wide boy saw me and you walking up to him, he already told himself we're the police before we said a word. Only way a brother and a white boy together – *got* to be the man. By the time he knew better, we're gone."

I nodded while he spoke. He was right. This business was all a matter of attitude.

He read my thoughts again. "You break an arm, a leg, whatever. It's no big deal, unless you let it be. You lay back, recuperate and wait for your opportunity. The right opportunity. This here, you jumping off half ready, it's not like you."

"I can't let this go."

Ron nodded. "Then find Eddie Reilly." He stood up. "I heard about Reds. I'm sorry."

I stood too. "Thanks. I appreciate that. I know you didn't care for him."

"I never said that. I said I didn't care for his approach – there's a difference."

I nodded.

Ron continued, "Redfern was always too much of a cowboy for my taste, but the man was a professional. I'll give him that." He nodded to his guys, and said to me, "Sit back down and finish your coffee. Make sure you say goodbye to Leonetta when you leave." He patted me on the back and said, "Don't be a stranger," then walked upstairs. The two guys followed.

I sipped at the coffee again; it had cooled. It was harsh, but strong, and the caffeine would help a lot.

I finished the cup and walked toward the door. Nobody looked at me, but everyone made a point of not being in my way. As I went by her, Leonetta said, "Hey," and reached across the bar. "I hope you feel better, soon."

I took her hand and said, "Thank you. And thanks for the coffee. It was delicious."

She walked away to wait on someone. I went outside, and looked at the note she'd slipped me – on it were four addresses.

21

I got into the Ford and loaded the Glock. I thought about Ron and the other gangsters I knew, and the games they had to play. They all believed that they lived by a code – that they would never reveal anyone else's secrets, they'd never rat. But they all did. It was how they survived. They gave up little pieces of information from time to time, to the police, to their rivals, and sometimes to guys like me. Giving it up through a third party was Ron's way of pretending it hadn't happened.

Philadelphia Police Headquarters takes up a city block, and shows off the plastic nature of concrete; its curved façade gently flows from the convex to concave and back. If you look at the building from the air, its outline describes an eccentric figure eight – or a set of handcuffs. I drove the Ford down Filbert Street and through the back gate to the parking lot, and nodded to a pair of cops in a wagon on their way out.

This was dicey. I'd told Armand that I'd be coming here. His unit was missing a car now. It had been dark in that alley, but those guys could still give him a pretty good description of what I looked like. I needed to speak to the Albanians while I could, before their lawyer found them and got them released. I peeled a hundred dollar bill loose from the wad I'd taken out of Brenda's apartment, rolled it into a tight cylinder and walked down the ramp to the basement door.

The turnkey on duty behind the Plexiglas looked up. She was sweating. The top three buttons of her dark gray uniform shirt were undone, revealing a good bit of cleavage, and the patch on the sleeve read, "Philadelphia Corrections Officer."

A cop at a desk down the hall to my left spoke on his phone. Somewhere deep inside the building someone was singing. I couldn't make out the tune.

I showed the guard Dougherty's badge and said, "You just get a couple of guys from The Fourteenth? Big dudes, foreign?"

She said, "Yeah. They're here."

"I'm working warrants. Those two know about a guy I'm looking for. Is there any way I can go back there and ask them a few questions?"

The woman looked uncomfortable. She shifted her bulk on the stool and said, "No, I don't know, man. I don't need get jammed up behind bullshit, you know?"

"This doesn't have anything to do with why they're here. Nobody will complain."

The guard looked pained. "I can't do that."

I looked around the vestibule; I didn't see a security camera but assumed there was one somewhere. I palmed the hundred-dollar bill I'd rolled and said, "Your nails look really nice. Did you get them done on Franklin Street?"

She was puzzled and held them up to look at them and said, "Thank you. No, not on Franklin Street. I go to the Korean place at Bridge and Pratt – "

"That really looks like the work they do over on Franklin Street. May I?" I reached though the slot and took her hand.

She was startled, but felt the bill and said, "Oh, yeah, I know the place you're talking about. For real? Franklin?"

I let go of her hand. "Yeah, Franklin. Check it out."

She said, "They do a nice job, there," reached inside her shirt and made as though she was adjusting her bra. "All right. You be on out of here in ten minutes."

"Okay."

"You know you still gotta check your piece?"

I nodded and she handed me a form. I carefully printed out the Glock's serial number. I knew places like this; I wanted to be sure I'd get back the same weapon. I took my copy, slid hers and the pistol to her and she buzzed me inside. "They all the way in the back."

It was dank and hot inside. The singing was clearer, but I didn't know the tune. It was an old man's voice. It wasn't too bad. I walked the length of the corridor. The cells were on my left. They were small rectangles, maybe five feet by eight, with a steel sink and toilet, and bare steel platform to sit or lie down on. More than half of them were occupied. Most of the prisoners were asleep or passed out. A stray fly buzzed me. The singer was in a cell halfway back – a skinny old man dressed only in a yellowed wife-beater and boxers. Blood had run down his face and crusted from an undressed wound on his scalp. His feet were scabbed and dirty. He stopped singing as I went by and said, "Hey. When y'all cutting me loose from here?" He said a lot more but I walked on and didn't listen.

The two were in separate, adjoining cells. The one with the neck tat said, "Look. Here is tough guy. Hello again, tough guy."

I said, "Who are the guys in the red van?"

They both turned toward the metal cell divider separating them, as though they might be able to see each other through it. The second guy said, "Fuck you."

"You two are stupider than I thought. I had you sent here. I can get you moved around all night if I want to."

"We have lawyer—"

"You have a lawyer who won't find you for hours. Who are the guys in the red van?"

"Lawyer is good." He put his face near the bars and shouted in the direction of the turnkey, "There be hell to pay once he finds us."

"He won't care about you two at all once he finds out that Anton is dead." They stared at me. I said, "Right. You didn't know that, did you?"

"No way."

I shrugged. "If I'm lying, it doesn't matter. If I'm not, it doesn't matter to me, but it will to you two. You're all alone, now."

They thought about that for a few moments and the first one said, "So what?"

"I'll tell you so what – a policeman was murdered last night because of all this." They were quiet. I continued, "Oh, yeah. You heard about that. I can tell a cop I know that you two did it, and he'll believe me. You'll never make it to the detention center. You'll be shot, trying to escape."

"Sure, a cop that listens to you. My ass."

"I got in here to talk to you, didn't I?"

The first one hadn't thought of that. Now, he looked worried. The second one licked his lips and said, "What do you want?"

"I want my money. I don't care about anything you're into." I let them think about that for a moment and said, "Who are the guys in the van?"

"We don't know names. The one guy Anton knows – does work with. One guy, he handles the peoples on boat and then comes with them in van. The other is new. Just come around to do some things. I think Anton doesn't like him. He was going to dump them both."

"Why?"

"Not – don't know why. Maybe Anton doesn't trusting them."

"What's your job with the people you smuggle in?"

"We expedite." He seemed proud to know that word.

"Could you expand on that?" He looked at me blankly. I said, "What does 'expedite' mean?"

"We meet them – take from contractor to places – restaurants, factories. Places that need workers. We collect moneys from places."

The other guy said, "We make things go smooth."

From the front desk, the turnkey hollered, "Y'all have to wrap it up."

"Two minutes." To the Albanians, I said, "What happened last night that has all you guys in a tizzie?"

"Huh?"

"Sorry. Why is everyone worried?"

"Why should we say?"

"If you help me, I'll help you. All I want is my money."

They looked in each other's direction again, and the first said, "The guys on boat last night think they see Coast Guard. They put everybody off boat. Anton hears. He was upset."

"They put the people into the river?"

"No, Port Authority Headquarters. Yes, into river, asshole."

"Where in the river?"

"They were not sure. Somewhere around Airport or Navy Yard."

This was a mess. "Did any of the people make it to shore?"

"They think maybe so. They go back later, in car, to try to look, but they were not knowing if they look in right places. Was dark. From river, things look different than from road."

The other said, "They stop looking in daylight. Too many police. They say they maybe go back again, later – tonight."

"Where haven't they looked yet?"

"Not sure. Most places along river hard to get to from road."

I didn't want to spend any more time here. "All right. Your lawyer will be here in a while." I started to walk away.

"Hey," one of them called out, "what we do now?"

I had no advice for them. I said goodnight to the turnkey and left.

22

I thought things over – by this point I'd all but given up on the hope of money inside Pastore's safe, but there might be some money for me in this somewhere – maybe with Reilly, maybe at Dougherty's place, if I could get back there.

I had to find Reilly. The addresses Ron had gotten me were spread around the city. The closest was just off Fairmount Avenue, half of a big, three-story brick twin with a mansard roof. Most of the homes in the block had been converted to apartments. There was evidence that this house had been left whole – there was only one electric meter on its side, no mailboxes in the vestibule, no separate doorbells. Dim light shown through every window.

I waited across the street, out of sight, about twenty feet down the block. In a few minutes two men got out of a car and went to the door and knocked. A guy opened the door and said, "What do you want?"

One of them said, "What do you think?"

The man looked them up and down and said, "I don't know you."

The other man said, "What? We look like a cops to you?"

"Everybody looks like cops to me."

The talker pulled up his shirt to expose his chest. "Is that enough? Or would you like to see more?"

"That's not my department." He opened the door the rest of the way and said, "You go on, enjoy yourselves." They entered and the door closed.

Getting inside wouldn't be difficult but searching the house would. I was too tired and felt too sick to fool around with this. It didn't seem likely that Reilly would choose to hide out in a cat house – there'd be too many people to depend on keeping quiet – but it wasn't impossible, either. I walked back toward the Ford.

A garden hose was coiled around a bracket fastened to the side of the second house, just forward of its side bay windows. I cut free about twelve feet and rummaged through a blue plastic recycling bin, took an empty wine jug with me back to the Ford, unscrewed the gas cap and ran the length of hose into the tank. Kneeling, I sucked on the free end of the hose a few times and got a mouthful of gas, and spit it out as I stuck the flowing end into the jug. It filled, and I pulled the hose free of the tank, popped the trunk and took the tire jack and a rag, along with the bottle of gasoline across the street to the rear of the whorehouse. I would have preferred kerosene – it's a lot safer – but it was difficult to find. Nobody used portable heaters much, anymore.

Ron was a friend, but he was an opportunist, too. It was possible that he was only using me to thin out his competition – his offer of work had put this latest idea in my head. I didn't have anything else though, and needed to be sure.

I jammed the rag into the neck of the jug, turned the bottle upside down to saturate it, and set the jug in the alley. With the jack, I bashed out a window close to the back door, lit the cloth and pitched the flaming bottle inside. It shattered and the room lit up immediately. I didn't need to wait and watch. The first floor rear of this house would soon be untenable. Nobody would be coming out of the back. I hurried around to the sidewalk.

From inside the house I could hear a few people yelling, and the door man rabbitted, sprinting down the front steps and away. Light smoke showed at the windows. A few seconds later the ladies and their patrons began to pour out of the entranceway, half dressed. Away from the fire they were busy pulling on shirts, working their feet into shoes. The smoke at the windows darkened. A first floor window on the side of the house stood open; the smoke thickened and little tongues of flame lapped out from the twisting plume. A few more people straggled out of the front door, some of the women crying, the men mostly annoyed. One complained, choking, "Hey, this is a rip-off. I want my money back."

There was a scream from above. I looked up; a bare-chested woman stood in a third floor window, calling for help. She crawled out the window as the smoke behind her intensified. She stood up on the mansard gutter and inched away from the window. Smoke from below obscured her from moment to moment. A fat guy dressed only in boxer shorts crawled out after her, hacking and coughing in the smoke. The height bothered him more than the fire; he stayed on his hands and knees and pressed himself back into the slate mansard face. I could hear glass breaking somewhere on the side of the house, and the sound of something hitting the ground. Flames were reflected in the windows of the house next door.

No one was paying any attention to me. I pushed my way through the crowd, turning the men toward me and looking at their faces. Reilly wasn't with them. I searched until I heard sirens and left. I still tasted gasoline. In the Ford, I took a mouthful of water from the bottle and spit it out the window.

*

The next address on Ron's list was an old four story, brick mill building. It appeared vacant. Its windows were tinned over with galvanized sheets. The building abutted a larger, six story factory structure, also empty, but even more neglected-looking. The façades of both were decorated with the works of local "artists," done in a variety of colored spray paints.

The front door was boarded shut. I got my fingertips under the panel, but it was tight to the doorframe, fastened with drywall screws. I could hear something from inside – very quiet, a kind of hum. I didn't think that Reilly would be here, either. Guys like him don't like to rough it. I still needed to see what was inside.

I walked around the building without finding access. In the rear was a steel roll-up door, and next to that a heavy steel, hinged entry door. Both looked new. I didn't try either.

In the building next to it there was an open exterior basement stairwell. Someone had bashed in the door; it hung askew, held up only by its bottommost hinge. Water pooled in the landing. I stepped over it and wrestled the door all the way open.

The basement stank. It was dark, but using my light might call attention that I didn't want. I searched for a stairway to the upper floors, feeling my way down a hallway strewn with debris, and stumbled over a mattress. Locals were using this place to fix and have sex. As I got deeper into the building my eyes adjusted. There were traces of light coming in from window wells on the far side of the building.

As I passed an open doorway I saw movement, and I ducked. Something whistled over my head, and clanged into the doorframe. I came up fast, punching, connecting twice with someone who grunted and fell, and dropped something metal that clattered across the concrete floor. I dragged the Glock from my waistband and racked a cartridge into the chamber.

A man said, "Don't do that. Please, brother." He sounded old. As he moved, I could make out his outline. I flicked on my penlight. He squinted in the glare, and could have been anywhere from thirty to eighty years old. On the floor next to him was a three-foot length of two-inch angle iron. He was frightened. "I don't need no trouble."

"Why are you making trouble for me, then?"

"I made a mistake. I thought you were somebody else, somebody tries to hurt me. Please, I didn't mean no disrespect."

"Get up and show me the stairs."

"You got it, brother. Let me get myself together." The bum made his way to his hands and knees and with difficulty, stood up. "Damn. You hit hard. I'll be pissing blood for a week."

He bent over and reached for the length of iron. I put my foot on it and said, "You won't need that."

"Right, you right." He straightened and took a step back.

"You help me out, I'll make it worth your trouble."

"That's a winner. You follow me, close. Down here's okay, but it's lots of holes in them floors upstairs, and steps missing and such."

He led the way through the corridor. I snapped off the light, picked up the metal bar and followed. My eyes adjusted to the dark again. I asked him, "Are there others in here? Somebody else who might make a mistake?"

"There's some in here, sure, but none that will trouble you. They know my walk. You'll be all right." He led the way into a stairwell. "Best keep close to the wall." He started up the first flight. "Stronger, there."

On the fifth floor, I looked across the building toward the windows overlooking the property I wanted. "How's the floor here?" I could make out the silhouette of collapse debris, outlined in the moonlight.

"Bad, this high up. Roof leaks, these here floors the most damaged." He began to pick his way across the floor, toward the windows. I followed him closely. Parts of the top floor had fallen in, creating obstacles.

At an open window frame, I saw that it was a six-foot drop to the slag roof next door. Twenty feet away was a hatch that covered the roof access to that building's interior.

I took out a twenty, tore it down the middle and held up half. "I might need help getting back inside here, okay?"

He took the half. "I know what you're saying, brother. I got you."

I dropped the length of angle iron out the window onto the roof, and let myself down as quietly as I could. The slag crunched under my shoes.

The hatch was wood, covered with tin, and coated with asphalt. I pulled at its corner; it gave a quarter-inch before it was fast on its hasps inside. I set the iron under its corner and pried up, bearing against the roof deck. Something gave, and I lifted the cover off its frame like it was hinged. Hot, stale air wafted up into my face.

A metal ladder was fastened to the wall of a stairwell. I could hear snoring as I climbed down. This floor was a large open loft space, filled with people – women, asleep on mats, sweating, in rows on the floor. A few were awake; I could make out muttered conversations from across the floor.

On the floor below that, there was activity, and the hum of motors. I crept down the stairs. Seated on benches at long tables were maybe three-dozen women, toiling at sewing machines. The women were mostly Asian, but a few white and black women were there, too, and some maybe from Latin America. A few were very young – girls, really – maybe eleven or twelve. It was dim here; save a few failing fluorescent tubes in ceiling mounts, the lighting came from small lamps set alongside the machines, forcing the women to sit hunched over, their faces close to the work. There were bundles of cut fabric, stacked near the seamstresses, and piles of rough, sewn garments. Most of the women appeared to be wearing clothes they had made here – cheap white blouses and light blue pants.

I walked the length of the tables. A few of the women looked up at me, and away. One stared. I said, to her, "Is this part of the new fall line?" She looked at me blankly.

There were thin partitions separating sections of the factory floor down here. On the other side of the wall, five women sweated over steam irons, pressing new, finished blouses. They hung the ironed garments on wheeled racks behind them.

One looked up at me. She was skinny and plain, and young, probably still in her teens. I could see that I frightened her, but there was something else in her expression. Maybe she still held out hope.

I heard sounds from the stairwell – male voices and footsteps coming up from the floor below. I held my finger to my lips. She nodded and went back to work. I hid myself behind a rack of clothes. Two men came out of the stairway and began to bark orders in some Asian language at the women ironing. One of the women spoke up, and got back-handed for her trouble. I saw an opportunity to buy back some goodwill from Armand. When the floor bosses moved on to the next room, I got the women's attention, held out my left hand, palm up and walked the fingers of my right across it. The woman who'd been slapped looked like she wanted to come, but stayed put, her eyes darting between the doorway to the next room and me. The skinny young girl nodded, put down her iron. An older woman next to her grabbed at her wrist and hissed, "Nah, nah," and other things that I couldn't understand. The younger woman yanked her arm away and came with me. The old lady kept it up until I turned and showed her the Glock. She shut up and went back to her iron. The other sat there, trembling, her cheek showing red where she'd been struck.

The girl tugged at my hand, frightened. Jobbers in places like this typically used fear of reprisals to keep the workers in line and on the job – threatening them, their co-workers, and family back home. Most of it was empty, but the threats were usually effective. This girl must have really wanted out.

She chattered at me under her breath until I stopped and placed my hand over her mouth. She was trembling – terrified – but nodded and stayed quiet. We ducked into the stairwell and I steered her up the stairs ahead of me. We climbed to the top floor, the ladder, and onto the roof. The air was cooler.

The bum helped me boost her up and into the window. "You got yourself a girlfriend, boss?"

"Shut up."

I kept my hand on the girl's upper arm, steering her past the bad spots in the floor, and we made our way downstairs and outside. I gave the bum the other half of the twenty.

I called Armand from the Ford while I drove. While the phone rang, I looked at the girl. They hadn't been pampering the help back there; as frightened as she was, she looked like she might fall asleep any moment. Her hands showed a number of cuts, and burn scars. There was a blood blister under the nail of her index finger. I handed her the bottle of water and she sucked down a third of it in one go. Armand picked up and I said, "Are you busy?"

"Yeah, I am, as a matter of fact. A couple of my geniuses let somebody scam them out of their city-owned vehicle. Are you familiar with the sentencing guidelines for GTA?"

I ignored all that and said, "If you aren't too busy, I got something for you." The girl watched me while I spoke.

Armand was quiet for a moment and said, "What?" He sounded tired.

"A sweatshop – clothing factory full of slaves – some of them kids."

"I can't do anything about that on your say-so. Not unless you'd like to come in and speak to a judge?"

"You're a funny guy. I can do one better. How about an escapee?"

"Does he speak English?"

"She. No. Does that matter?"

"It would help, but I can work with it. What does she speak?"

"I'm not sure." I looked at her in the passenger seat. "She's probably either Burmese or Thai."

"No matter. We'll figure it out."

"Good. I'll drop her off with the address and a note to call you."

"Drop her off where?"

"At one of the districts. You'll figure it out."

Armand laughed and hung up.

I headed toward the 22nd. Most police stations have a big poster in the lobby with a message offering help written in about thirty languages – "Point to your language and an interpreter will be called." She could pick out hers and eventually they'd find somebody who could talk to her and get her story – if she went inside, and if she hung around, and if she could read.

She still looked pretty scared. As I drove I thought about talking to her – she wouldn't know what I was saying but speaking to her in a calm voice might make her feel better – but I knew that somebody else had probably spoken to her like that, along the way to making her push a steam iron for the rest of her life. Added to that, I was too tired, and honestly had no idea what would happen to her once Armand got what he wanted. I stayed quiet the rest of the ride.

I scribbled my note for Armand and handed it to her, leaned past her to open the passenger door and pointed at the police station. She got out and walked across the sidewalk. I pulled away without watching to see if she went inside. She probably would; she had nowhere else to go.

23

Those places may have belonged to Pastore, but Reilly hadn't been in either of them. None of this was helping. I was getting tired of doing Ron's dirty work, but I didn't have much else, so I pressed on. I considered skipping to the fourth address on the list, but Ron may have thought of that, too.

The third address was a house just north of Old City, with a for sale sign fastened to the front stoop's iron railing. I noticed black specks in the front windows – flies, gathered on the inside of the windowpanes— dozens of them milling around.

I tried the door. The deadbolt was unfastened – there was some play as I shook the door in its frame – but the knob was locked. It was an older design and opened easily.

The air inside the house was foul. I stood there for a few moments and listened. There was no sound but the buzzing of the flies.

The place had been gone through. Closets, cabinets and drawers everywhere stood open or pulled out, but the searcher had been frustrated – like Pastore's boat, there were no contents. This house had been readied for sale – cleaned up and painted, new appliances and carpet – but hadn't yet been sold or rented out.

I went into the kitchen. It was the same: all the cabinet doors stood open and the shelves pulled out and on the floor. Flies crawled across the gray granite countertop. The oven door hung open. The trivets had been dropped onto the floor and the stovetop propped up. The refrigerator door was closed. I took a breath and pulled it open. The light bulb inside it popped on, showing it empty of contents. A fly lit on my cheek. I slapped at it but missed. I closed the door on the glare and waited for my eyes to become accustomed to the dark again. That's when I noticed the back door looked funny. The molding near the deadbolt was splintered. The door had been kicked in. Someone had done their best to make it look closed, but it hung askew. I went upstairs.

A dead man was in the back bedroom, lashed with duct tape to a wooden kitchen chair. His head hung down. Blood had dripped from his face to his lap. There were cigarette burns on the back of his neck. On the floor by his feet were six or seven teeth, bloody roots showing red against the carpet. The only movement was from the flies crawling over his body.

I supposed this was Reilly but needed to be certain. I grabbed him by his hair and pulled his head up. The flies took off, scattering, bumping against my arms and face. It was him – eyes wide open, his face frozen into a surprised grimace. His nose had been broken, pushed sideways. His tongue had swollen and stuck beyond his protruding front teeth – the teeth that were still in his mouth. There were bloody spaces where they'd been yanked out. I let go and his head slumped back over.

He hadn't talked before he'd died. Whoever did this wouldn't have torn the place apart if Reilly had told them about what they were looking for. It seemed this was a case of the questioners being over-zealous. They either hadn't known about his asthma, or he'd choked to death on his own blood. I doubted they'd found what they wanted, either. The search looked busy but not thorough. Amateur.

I had wasted a lot of time looking for Reilly – looking for answers that I wouldn't be getting. I thought it out. Reilly wasn't in the life but he was a smart guy. He'd need more than his word to sell to the investigators if it came to that – he'd need hard evidence – something he could put his hands on quickly. If he'd spooked and had to get out of the house, he wouldn't want to run back upstairs for something. It also wouldn't likely be anything big, or difficult to either hide or run with. It probably wouldn't even be in the house. Here, he'd have something smaller, like a key. I patted him down and went through his pockets. They were empty.

I started looking on the second floor anyway, just to be thorough. I went through the room he was in, and in the rest of the bedrooms, taking off switch plates, vent covers, looking for loose edges in the wall-to-wall carpet. I cut Reilly loose of the tape to free the kitchen chair, and stood on it to check out the overhead light fixtures.

In the bathroom, I looked in the toilet tank, unscrewed the strainer from the faucet, and took apart the trap. I stood on the chair and pulled down the surround and glass from the recessed hi-hat lamp in the ceiling, removed the bulb and felt around inside the housing.

I moved downstairs. Reilly would think like a straight-arrow – he'd expect trouble to come knocking at the front door. He'd plan to go out the back.

I went into the kitchen again. A receptacle above the counter top was missing its screw. I pulled free the cover plate; it had been fixed there with putty. Jammed inside the box was an AMTRAK baggage claim ticket.

24

I needed to check a few things before I went to the train station. At Jefferson University Hospital, I badged a security guard at the main entrance, and a nurse at the E.R. desk, and said to her, "I'm looking for a man, brought in here last night by Fire Rescue. He was in a car wreck. I think that he has a head injury. Does any of that sound familiar?"

"Yeah, that does. Hold on a minute," to another nurse farther down the counter, she said, "Nadine, what happened with that guy, you know, the MVA?"

"I think he's in the ICU."

I said, "Can you make sure? Or should I ask at the main desk?"

"No, I can find out for you." She typed on a keyboard and looked at the computer screen. "He's not there anymore. His X-Rays and EEGs were normal and they moved him to a room, Eight Thirty-Three."

"Thanks. Is he conscious? Can he answer questions yet?"

"I'm sorry, you won't be able to see him tonight. The orders are very definite."

I said, "That's disappointing," but smiled and added, "Okay. My relief will see him in the morning." She turned to ask the other woman something, and I said, "I'm sorry, is there a men's room I can use?"

"Yes, just down the hall."

She went back to work. I went past the rest room, followed exit signs around the corner and into the hospital proper. Next to a bank of elevators was a doorway marked "Stairs." I took them down to the basement.

The hallways here were tight, jammed with the building's guts; the walls and low ceiling were lined with pipes, conduits and cables. In addition to conventional utilities, the basement housed the systems that provided fire protection alarms, sprinklers and medical grade oxygen. The physical plant played a monotonous, dissonant symphony.

I found a locker room and went inside, and heard gentle snoring. In the last row of lockers was an old black man, asleep in a molded, plastic chair, his head slumped forward, arms folded across his lap, legs crossed at the ankle. He was dressed in blue coveralls. Around his neck hung a lanyard and clear plastic sheath with an ID card in it. I lifted it whole over his head without disturbing him, and looked around the locker room.

In a laundry cart, along with clean sheets and towels, was a pile of clean, thin blue coveralls marked "Environmental Services" over the left breast pocket. I grabbed two, put one on over my clothes and slung the ID tag around my neck. Checking lockers, looking into the open ones, I found a brown Jeff hat and put it on, too. It still felt damp from last evening's rainstorm.

I needed something else, something to distract someone, to keep them from looking at my face. I prowled around the basement, looking in rooms, until I found one with a workbench. On top was a white cloth nail apron. I tied it around my waist. There was a plastic five-gallon bucket under the bench half-full of oil dry. I dumped it, and rummaged through the bench drawers and found some tools, put the spare coveralls and tools in the bucket, and took the elevator to the eighth floor. The car stopped on the third floor and a fat nurse got on. I said, "Which floor?" and readied myself to punch the button.

She said, "Six."

I pushed it and said, "There you go."

She said, "Y'all aren't supposed to use this here. Y'all supposed to use the freight elevator."

I said, "I'm new," and turned away from her. She got off when the door opened and I continued to the eighth floor.

I went to the nurse's station on the floor and said to the woman on duty, "We got a bad leak on the floor below. I got to take a look around, see if something's running up here."

The nurse looked confused. "I don't know. There isn't anybody –"

"Yeah, yeah, I know, but we got big problems downstairs. Water's running all over the power lines, and computer stuff. I won't disturb anybody."

"I can't leave the desk."

"That's okay, I know my way around the building." I walked down the hall without looking back. I hoped that she'd fret until I was out of sight and forget about me.

The rooms here were doubles. Inside each, men and women were lying flat on their backs, hooked up to machines. Everywhere were tiny dots of light from LEDs, and the beeps of monitoring equipment.

Dougherty was in the second bed, close to the window. I had to use my penlight to check his face and still almost didn't recognize him, and needed to check for his name on the band around his wrist. His head was swathed with white gauze dressings. His nose was splinted and his eyes had dark rings around them. Pads and wires led from his exposed chest to a monitor near his bed. Hung from a stand next to that, an IV bag dripped liquid through a line and needle stuck into the crook of his right arm. I shook him. "Dougherty. Wake up."

The guy in the bed next to him snored and tried to roll over.

I shook Dougherty again, harder, and he came around. He stared at me for a few seconds, grimaced and mumbled something unintelligible, and said, "What do you want?"

"Where's my safe?"

"Huh?" He stared at me and his eyelids began to shut. I pressed my knuckles into his sternum and rubbed hard until he complained. I repeated, "Where's my safe?" He stared at me. I said, "You still have a chance to walk away from all of this. You're here as a John Doe. You can skip out of here before the police come back to talk to you, but you have to tell me what's going on or I'll see to it you're fucked. What's it going to be?"

He still seemed rocky, but said, "What do you want?"

"My safe. The guys in the van took it. Who are they?"

"I only know the one. I don't know anything about the safe."

"The one you know – that would be Brenda's little brother?"

He looked pained but said, "Yeah."

"You met Brenda through Pastore, right?"

He nodded and tried to push himself up in the bed, stretching the leads. "I'd like to get through this, man. Could you – "

"Not yet. How long have you and Pastore done things for each other?"

"I don't know. A while."

"What do those guys have planned for him?"

"I don't know."

"Joe, do you know what happens to cops who go to prison?"

"I'm not a cop."

"No, you're worse – you're one step up the ladder from being a turnkey. They'll take you apart in the big house." I let him picture that and said, "Brenda's brother took the safe from George. Why are they still coming after me?"

"Look, that guy, he – he doesn't say anything much to me."

"You're lying."

"No, no, really. He's a scary kid. You say hello to him, he doesn't answer. He stares at you like you don't exist and then turns away."

The guy in the next bed snorted and moaned. I tried another angle. "Why'd she tell you to watch Pastore's house?"

The change in subject threw him. He was trying to think of a way around the answer until I said, "Joe, you aren't smart enough to lie to me convincingly." He looked lost. I helped him focus "She and her brother are with the guys bringing people into the country, right."

He nodded.

"What's any of this got to do with Pastore?"

Dougherty looked around the room and said, "Something happened the night before last. They're all trying to clean it up. She asked me to help out."

"This would be the thing on the river?"

He balked – surprised – and said, "Yeah.

"What's it got to do with me?"

"I don't know. Honest, they didn't say, they just asked me to – to follow you – see where you went, that's all."

"You were supposed to use me to find Marcolina and anyone else, right?"

He hesitated and said, "Yeah."

"And then you were going to kill us. You or Scott."

He was going to deny it but just said, "Not me, I – look, I'm sorry, man."

"Why? It doesn't make sense. He's got the safe, why not let it go and take care of his business?"

"He thinks we're all better off just taking you out of the game. He said he thought you were too dangerous. After they finished with you and Marcolina, Scott and those other guys were gonna go back down around the airport, there, and look around."

"Look for what?"

"I don't know. Look, I'm not sure, ok? Honest."

I took out the writ I'd taken from him. "What about this?"

"Right." He pushed himself up in the bed again, and straightened out the IV line. "D'Allesandro is getting Pastore sprung. The judge signed that and plans to call the Detention Center at six this morning. I was going to make the pick-up then and take him away."

"Then what?"

Out in the hall, an elevator door opened. I stared at Dougherty and put my finger to my lips. He looked toward the door but stayed quiet. Footsteps sounded, moving away down the hall.

I repeated, "Then what?"

He swallowed and said, "I was gonna make like I was taking Pastore to the judge's house." He lay there, trying to think for a few moments. Then he gave up and said, "Something is supposed to happen along the way."

"Let me guess – you're supposed to get waylaid. This guy Scott would shoot Pastore, but you wouldn't get hurt, right? Maybe you'll just get hit on the head? To make it look good? I suppose you have a story all ready for the cops, what happened, what the shooter looked like, right?"

Dougherty was hesitant. "Yeah. So what?"

"All of that sounds reasonable to you?"

He looked at me blankly. His stupidity annoyed me so I punished him a little bit more. "You're a Sheriff's Deputy, so the police will believe your story, and say too bad for Pastore, and you go on your way, right?" He still didn't get it. "Brenda must be a hell of a piece of ass to get you to do all this."

"Hey, I don't like – "

"She's breaking up with you, Joe."

He just lay there, trying to think it through. I gave it up and said, "You're an idiot. The guy is going to shoot you, too. He'll probably shoot you first – you'd be armed."

"No, no, they wouldn't do that. They have a good thing with me – Brenda wouldn't – she – I have –" His objections ran down as he began to realize that I was right. It was sad to watch.

"Where does D'Allesandro live?"

He swallowed and said, "I'd like to get through this."

"We all would." I let him think about that and said, "Where does the judge live?"

Dougherty said, " Eighteen Twenty-Three Delancey Street." He looked down at himself. "How can I get out of here?"

I opened a cabinet and found some gauze and tape and then pointed to the monitor and said, "What is that?" He turned to look and I yanked the IV line out of his arm.

"Ow!" He clamped his hand over the wound.

"Shut up." I gave him the dressing and tape. "Cover that." I shut off the monitor, pulled the leads off his chest and gave him the spare coveralls and the hat. "Put these on, go down the stairs to the basement and walk out the loading dock. Walk a couple blocks away, then take a cab home, take the bandages off your head, change your clothes and call your supervisor," I cut his wristband off with my penknife, "Tell him you got mugged – the robber got your badge and gun – and you got hit in the head and need to go off sick. If he tells you to go to the hospital, go, but don't come back to this hospital." Dougherty stared at me, insulted, and went back to bandaging his arm. "If they want to start a line or take your blood pressure, don't show them that arm. Can you remember all that?" He nodded and stayed quiet. He was trying to think. I held up his badge and said, "You try to fuck me, and I'll make sure this turns up somewhere ugly – somewhere you don't talk your way out of."

He seemed to collapse inward. "Okay." He knew he was stuck. "Okay. I'll do it your way."

"That's good. Tell your boss and whoever else needs to know that you never saw anybody. They hit you from behind." I gave him his house keys.

He got out of bed, slowly. "What about Pastore's papers? I don't know if I show on any of it –"

"None of it will go public. Me and you, we'll work something out."

He stepped into the coveralls. His shoes were on the floor in the closet.

There were footsteps coming down the hall in our direction. I said, "I'll get rid of whoever this is and then you go."

"But – but what about –"

"I'll be in touch, Joe."

I walked out of the room, carrying the bucket of tools. The nurse from the desk was coming toward me and said, "I called downstairs. There's no leak down there. What are you doing in here?"

I walked past her saying, "Yeah, I must have gotten off on the wrong floor. Everything's ok up here," and got into the elevator. She was saying something that I didn't pay attention to as the door closed.

At the ground floor reception desk, a nurse and the sleepy maintenance man from the basement were talking to a uniformed security guard. He spoke to me on my way out. "Were you up on the eighth floor?"

I tried to move past him, "Yeah, I'll be back. I'm getting something to eat."

He put a hand up and blocked my way. "I'm going to have to see your ID." He squinted, trying to look at the picture on the lanyard.

Normally I'd have talked my way past this man, but I was tired and sore, and didn't have the patience I should. I pointed to the door and said, "Here comes my boss. Talk to him."

As he turned, I kicked him in the side of the knee. He went down hard. "Ow!"

I grabbed him by the hair and bounced his head on the floor. He went glassy-eyed and tried to grab at my hand but I was already up and moving. The woman stared, and the old man made to say something. I gave them both a hard look and went out the revolving door.

I came outside onto 11th Street. There was a rainbow emblem under the numerals on the street sign. I walked north. Ahead of me, two men exited a bar named Woody's Playhouse and crossed the street, heading in the direction of a building that was visible through a parking lot, with the word Voyeurs projected across its façade. The two looked familiar. I caught up to them and said, "Hi, fellas."

Marcolina looked frightened but Larry was delighted. "Oh, my. Your outfit is priceless." He felt the fabric of my coverall sleeve between his thumb and forefinger. "It's a tragedy that we can't return to Gabriel's – he'd just love it. You seemed much too butch for costumes, friend. Why the change of heart?"

I threw my arm around Marcolina's shoulder but spoke to Larry: "Where did you two disappear to?" I turned to Marcolina and said, "We have a lot to talk about."

"Hey, look, man, we had to get out of there. That was a really bad scene – I'm no hard guy. I put you together with Brenda – I figured you had everything from me that you needed and I'd hear from you later. That's all."

"I wasn't too happy being left there."

"I'm sorry, I was scared. You're right, I'm sorry. I shouldn't have left you. I was scared, man."

Larry said, "If it means anything, it was I who suggested that it was time for us to leave. Mickey recalled that he had a hide-a-key stuck up under his passenger side fender. Brenda also felt that it was time to go."

"Where is Brenda?"

Marcolina said, "I dropped her off a little ways away from the party, at a club in East Falls. She said she needed to talk to somebody. I guess she went home after that, but I don't know."

Larry pointed over his shoulder at the club. "Please, let's go inside and sit at a table like civilized people. I'm parched."

I considered and said, "Okay. Do I need a membership card?"

"Not at all. Follow me."

A big, bald man with a handlebar mustache let us inside. It was crowded. A dozen or so young men were dancing to bad club music, but most of the patrons were seated, having drinks. Two or three customers said hello to Larry. Only a few others paid any real attention to us. We sat at a table near the back that was partially occupied by a couple too busy to notice us.

A waiter said to Larry, "Hello, dear heart. Who are your friends?" He put coasters on the table in front of us.

"This is Mickey, and this is," he looked at me questioningly.

I looked at the ID lanyard around my neck and said, "Henry Meadows."

The waiter said, "And what should we call you? Henry? Hank?"

"You can call me Mister Meadows."

He laughed and said, "I'm going to have to keep my eye on you," and took our orders. The couple didn't want anything.

I stripped off the ID and coveralls as I said to Marcolina, "Woody's – here – I didn't realize you swung this way, man." I wadded up the coveralls and dropped them on the floor.

Larry chuckled, "I've been doing my best to turn this man out for ages."

Marcolina was tired. "Please. I figured it would be a good way of staying scarce."

"So you haven't been doing anything helpful, you've just been hiding out?"

"I've been keeping myself from getting hurt."

I said, "This life isn't for tourists. You have to decide if you're in or you're out and act accordingly."

Larry interrupted me, saying, "Whatever are you talking about, friend?"

To him, I said, "Butt out." To Marcolina, "Do you understand me?"

He looked serious and nodded, then said, "Have you gotten any closer to the money?"

"No. I'm getting the impression there never was any."

He looked disgusted. "Great."

"Your outcome isn't a total loss. You don't owe Anton anything, not anymore."

He looked confused, and made to speak but stopped and nodded.

A pair of uniformed cops came into the bar and spoke to the bartender, who pointed toward our table. The dancers stopped dancing. Everyone in the bar was watching the cops as they walked toward us. I kicked the coveralls behind me. The older of the two cops, a skinny black man said, "May I see some identification, gentlemen?" The younger cop, a white kid, glanced around the club, trying not to stare at anyone, and self-consciously tugged at his uniform and hat. The dancers moved a few steps toward our booth. The couple finally came up for air and frowned at the police.

Larry said loudly, "Oh, this is exciting. What are we supposed to say now? 'What's wrong officer? Was I speeding?'"

The patrons within earshot laughed. Someone called out, "I like the young one."

Another said, "Oh no you don't, girlfriend, I saw him first."

The young cop reddened. Another pair got up from their table and moved toward us.

The black cop began to say something, but a customer yelled, "Don't worry, poppa, someone will ask you to dance."

He looked around and said, "One more word and I'll call for a wagon."

Three or four patrons said, "Ooh!" and giggled.

The cop looked back at us and said, "IDs on the table. Now."

Marcolina had his wallet out. "Officers, I'm an attorney." He produced a business card and handed it to the older cop. "Seriously, you don't want to make a mistake here."

The cop looked at the card and said, "Thank you for the advice, counselor," and tossed the card away.

A few of the other patrons didn't like that. The young cop wiped a bead of sweat off his forehead and re-seated his hat. The waiter caught his eye and blew a kiss at him.

Larry said, "I insist that you tell us what this is all about, tiger."

The older cop spoke to Larry while he stared at me, "A security guard was assaulted at Jefferson Hospital. We believe the perpetrator came into this establishment. You," he pointed at me, "ID, now."

A patron said, "This is harassment."

One of the couple at our table said, "We've been here for hours."

The other giggled and said, "We can vouch for each other," and stuck his tongue in the first's ear. The young cop blanched.

I showed the older cop the backs of my hands. "Do I look like I've assaulted anyone?"

It only made him more curious about me. He said, "I'm not going to ask you again." He rested his hand on the flap of his holster.

A few of the customers called out that I didn't have to show them anything.

The cop raised his voice and said to the crowd, "You people had best shut your mouths and back off."

Someone said, "Oh, so now it's 'you people,' huh?" The crowd inched closer.

I stared at the cop while I reached into my pocket and slowly brought out Dougherty's wallet, laid it on the table and flipped it open to show the badge and ID.

The cop said, "Get the fuck out of here. You're a sheriff's deputy? Let me see that."

His partner was watching the rest of the bar patrons surrounding us. "Hey, Cleve, maybe we should call for some assistance, you think?"

"You keep your hand off that radio." Cleve was annoyed. He hadn't wanted to come into this bar but he was here and he was old-school; you didn't call for help as soon as things got difficult, you handled it. His squad would never let him hear the end of it if he couldn't deal with a bar room full of gay men.

To the crowd he shouted, "Back off, now. I won't say it again." The patrons ignored him. To me he said, "Deputy, let me see your ID."

Someone goosed the young cop from behind. He whirled around, and another customer grabbed his ass. He jumped, and mouthed a few things but stayed mute. The crowd laughed at his discomfort.

I said to the older cop, "That's Deputy Sergeant."

He beckoned for the wallet with his fingers, palm up. "Let's go, Sergeant."

I stood up and handed it to him. He inspected it and said, "This ain't you."

I said loudly, "What are you trying to say, officer – that there's some kind of law against a gay man being a sergeant in the Sheriff's Department? Is that what this is?" I turned, speaking to the patrons, who by now were complaining loudly and had formed a tight circle around us, and were jostling the cops, "I thought we were past all of the bashings and harassment, but I suppose I was wrong – the police can just come walking in here and push us around anytime they want."

The crowd overwhelmed the policemen. I gave up on getting back Dougherty's wallet, and pushed my way past the throng, toward the door. The cops had their hands full. A customer in a sleeveless T-shirt had snatched the young cop's uniform hat, and was wearing it sideways. My last look at the older cop told me that he wished he'd let the young guy make that call.

I went outside and grabbed a cab that was going by. I didn't want to push my luck with the Ford any farther, either. I'd asked Armand a few questions about Judge D'Allesandro. It would be like him to put a man somewhere near her house to see if the car turned up there.

25

The judge lived on a tree-lined block. Sycamore roots skewed the flagstone pavement. I didn't see anyone watching. The second time I pushed the bell, a light came on upstairs. A minute later I heard the security chain engaged and the front door opened a few inches. Judge D'Allesandro looked through the gap at me and said, "I've got 911 on the line." She showed me the phone and let me mull that over for a moment. "What do you want?"

"George Rafferty, the retired cop who got shot last night – I've got information. I'll give it to you alone."

"Are you surrendering yourself?"

"Hardly. Hang up the phone, your honor. I'm no danger to you."

She was wary. "Why come to me? Why not go to the police?"

"Please, don't insult me."

She hesitated, and spoke into the phone, "I don't think that I'll be needing anything tonight. Thank you." She ended the call and said to me, "What do you know about Mister Rafferty?"

"I'm not going to talk to you out here. Invite me in." She was hesitant. "You're in a lot of trouble. I'm trying to help you."

She stood her ground. "What makes you think I need help?"

"The writ you signed to have Senator Pastore released from custody this morning, for one."

She blanched, and said, "All right," closed the door to undo the chain and re-opened the door fully. "Come inside." I stepped into the vestibule and she said, "What do you want?" The judge was a tall, attractive woman in her early forties. She was wearing a robe, but it was clear she'd been awake for a while.

"I want the safe that I took out of Pastore's home. If somebody has already opened it, I want its contents."

"What's any of that got to do with me?"

"Don't waste my time, your honor. It has everything to do with you. What does he have on you?"

She composed herself and said, "Vic Pastore has been involved in court business over the years. I have made some judgments favorable to him. Come in and sit." She went over to a liquor cabinet. "Drink?"

As she spoke, she seemed familiar to me – as though I'd met her before. I said, "No, and you don't want one either." Out of habit, I glanced around the room. She had a lot of nice things. "What about these court cases?" An ebony curio cabinet caught my eye.

"There is nothing that I've done that is illegal, but with everything and everyone liable to be named in Vic's papers, some of what I've done might be considered unethical. I would spend a lot of time explaining myself. Time I don't have. Sit down, please." She sat in a leather Eames chair and continued, "There's an opening coming up in the state supreme court at the end of the year, and I want it."

I walked to the cabinet. Among other things inside it was a green-glass perfume bottle and stopper. On the silver medallion was engraved the Monogram DDM. I said, "You're George's sister-in-law."

She saw what I was looking at and said, "You've been to his house. Jeanie has one just like mine. Yeah, my father gave all the girls those when we graduated from high school." She seemed to soften. "He was a dear man, my father."

"So you're George's 'friend.' You told him about Pastore's legal troubles?"

"Yes." She got business-like. "Please, sit down."

I did. "How close are you to Pastore?"

"What do you want to know?"

"Just what I asked."

"We are old friends. That's all."

"You never dated him?"

"We've gone on dates, but no, we've never dated." She met my stare and said, "Vic really isn't interested in girls. He and Eddie Reilly – why are you asking?"

"I'm just trying to get a sense of how far you'd go."

She was lost.

I said, "You think you'd still get that judgeship after Pastore got shot this morning?"

"What are you talking about?"

"That was the plan. Pastore was never going to make it here."

"That wasn't – " She was trying to think it through. "That wasn't what I wanted."

"What did you want?"

"A deal. Sometimes Vic and I help each other, and sometimes we don't. Vic's crapped out this time, and I don't want to let him take me down, too." She picked at her robe. "I was going to offer him help, in exchange for leaving me out of his mess."

"That's a stretch. You wouldn't have to spring him for that. You could tell him all that at the Detention Center." I added, "Springing him at six in the morning? The timing is unusual."

"The government's case is weak – he's broken the law, certainly, and he'll be found guilty, but this circus – his incarceration – is the result of an over-zealous federal prosecutor's desire to make a name for himself." She continued in an official sounding voice, "Once I realized how flimsy the government's evidence was, I didn't want to see my longtime friend and colleague languish a moment more than necessary."

I took the writ out of my pants pocket and unfolded it carefully; it was wet and threatened to tear. "Anybody looking at this after he got shot wouldn't see it that way."

"You're blackmailing me?"

"No. I apologize if I gave that impression. Blackmail is an amateur's game. I'm a professional. I want to give you this. Tell me who told you to write it."

"Nobody tells me to do anything."

"Less than ethical behavior by a Philadelphia judge is so commonplace you'd be suspect if you hadn't. That wouldn't keep you off the state supreme court. No, there's got to be more. Somebody told you to sign that writ. Who?"

"Nobody. I – "

"Okay. We're done." I stood up, folding the writ.

"Wait. All right, will you wait? It was Brenda Michaels."

I put the writ down on her coffee table. "How do you know Brenda?"

"I've known her forever. I got her the job she has now." She thought for a moment and continued, "Brenda had a really easy time in school. We both had to work our way through, but she never had a problem with any of the homework." She paused and said, "I did. Once I got into college, I was swamped. Brenda helped me out, sometimes –"

"She wrote your term papers."

"How did you – " Her surprise was genuine. "Yes. She did, but she didn't do it for nothing. I couldn't keep up with the workload and wait tables at the same time. She wrote most of my essays and term papers. Did it for others, too. It was how she worked her way through school. She kept it up after her mother died and she had to drop out." The judge's expression changed. "Two nights ago, she showed me pencil copies of some of them, in one of those black composition books, and said she needed me to get Vic released."

"You did this over homework?"

"Proof of plagiarism in college would ruin my chances for that seat. It could ruin my career."

"How is she compromised? I understand what Pastore has on you and that idiot Sheriff's Deputy, but what about her?"

She laughed. It was a pleasant laugh, but it didn't suit her expression. "Why, you're just a babe in the woods, aren't you?"

"I don't follow you."

"That's just my point. You seem like a fairly smart guy but you miss a lot." She paused, and saw that I was annoyed and decided not to push it. "Nobody has anything on Brenda. She isn't bailing out of anything."

I saw it now: Brenda was taking over – eliminating the competition. I nodded and said, "It's been a long night."

She reached for the writ. I chuckled and said, "No, we aren't doing things that way," got up and walked to the kitchen.

She followed. "What are you doing?"

I flipped the switch for the range hood and turned a stove knob. A burner sparked and lit up. She said, "Oh."

I set fire to the writ, twisting it in my hand so it would consume itself, and dropped the last flaming bit into the sink.

I said, "You take care of yourself, your honor," and made my way to the door.

"Hey."

I turned.

"I hope that you're not leaving here with the impression that I could help you if you ever end up in my courtroom."

"I'll be disappointed if things ever get that far along. Good night."

26

I handed a Redcap the baggage claim. A few minutes later he came back with a black carry-on suitcase, the kind with an extension handle and wheels. I tipped him ten bucks, rolled the case to the empty station diner and took a seat in a booth. I ordered coffee from the tired waitress, hoisted the case onto the bench seat, and opened it. There were a few changes of clothes – shirts, slacks, underwear and socks, a pair of shoes and a shaving kit. One of the inside pockets was full; there were seven thousand dollars in hundreds.

I went through the shaving kit. There was a razor, toothpaste and brush, floss, a bar of soap in a plastic case, a comb and brush, an inhaler, and three brown plastic prescription bottles. So he did have asthma.

Under all that was a hardbound ledger and some legal envelopes full of papers. I paged through the ledger; there were rows of initials, numbers in columns, dates amounts, and notes under "remarks," like, "Call and thank," and "Difficult. Give this to J. D." I supposed that meant Joe Dougherty. Or maybe Judge D'Allesandro. It didn't matter. The envelopes were full of contracts and proposals, and things like that. There were a lot of things here that might be helpful to the prosecutor, but nothing that would help me.

This was Reilly's run-out bag. He'd thought ahead, keeping it stashed here – easier to get out of town by rail than air – but he never made it.

I put it all back together and went out into the terminal, found a Redcap and put the bag into storage again.

I caught the 4:29 train on the Airport High-Speed Line to the terminals, hopped on a shuttle and took it to Avis. Dougherty had been too dazed or too dumb to cancel his cards. I still had his Visa, and used it to rent a mid-sized sedan. I skipped the insurance. The counter girl snapped her gum and admonished me to come back with a full tank of gas. "You do *not* want to pay the company's prices. Believe me."

I thanked her and drove to the exit, then to Island Avenue. I pulled over and checked the dome light; it had a switch. I opened the door and shut it off.

The river's frontage along the city was huge, but from what the Albanians had told me, I decided to take a chance on the guys in the van searching the waterfront near the airport. There was a lot of acreage, with only one way in or out, and brush was deep there. If this was a matter of Brenda and her brother cutting out the middlemen, I could see that they might be paranoid about a survivor of last night's debacle living to tell their story. I picked a spot off the highway to pull over, and waited. I felt myself starting to nod and dry-swallowed two more Excedrin. The airport tower was visible through the mist off to my right. A plane arced overhead; it seemed that I could reach out and scratch the belly of the big jet – it looked that close.

I'm not sure how much time passed before I saw them, turning off onto Island Avenue. I followed. When they turned onto Hog Island Road, I shut my headlights off and turned in behind them. The road was a poorly maintained, two-lane macadam that cut through marshy ground, thick with junk trees and bramble, and roughly paralleled the airport's southern fence, but it had been built along pathways that predated the airport itself, and so was tricky; there were lots of twists and curves. I needed to follow the van closely enough that I wouldn't miss them turning off, but not so close that they'd see me. The only other vehicles likely to be out here now were Airport cops. I shut off the A.C. and rolled the windows down, in an effort to hear their engine. Through gaps in the woods to my left, I could see lights on the river – a fuel barge off-loading Jet-A, the terminal and its tank farm.

In places here, the river had exceeded its banks. A long stretch of the road was flooded. Water covered an expanse of marsh to my left as far as I could see. The water in front of me was moving – sloshing back and forth in the rebound of the van's wake. I slowed to a crawl. The water came up to the axles. Once through, I picked up speed and nearly missed them; they had turned onto a gravel service road. I waited two beats and followed. It was a straight shot along this road to the river. They'd hear me once they shut off the van's engine, so I unlatched the door and held it open with my left hand while I rolled along behind them. When their brake lights flashed, I killed the ignition and coasted to a stop without touching the brake, and got out of the car soundlessly.

I'd prefer to have them both talking, but that would be tricky, and the driver shot too well to allow him another opportunity. Standing crouched behind the open door, I braced the back of my hand against the windshield frame, sucked in a breath and held it, while I drew a bead on the space just outside the driver's side door. As he stepped out of the van, I fired twice. He fell and didn't move. The passenger was out and running before I could adjust. I snapped a shot in his direction, but missed; he was away, through the weeds. I ran around the Buick and followed.

He moved well for a stocky guy. Something about him looked familiar. As he ran through the brush, I was just able to keep him in sight – the motion more than anything else. I could hear him as well, until another jet roared overhead. I lost him.

Ahead of us was a clearing, and a long, low commercial building – windowless – some sort of support business for the airport. There were about a dozen cars behind a high chain-link fence in a dimly lit parking lot. I stopped just short of the edge of the wood and listened.

I was rewarded: He was climbing the fence, maybe in the hopes of stealing a car and driving away. I fired another shot in his direction. He dropped to the ground and ran. In the light, I saw that he was Jimmy Florio.

He ran back toward the river, past the airport. I chased him through the head-high weeds, easily following his trail of crushed growth. Ahead of us were two prefab steel buildings fronting the river, each a hundred feet deep, one vacant, the other refitted and occupied as a self-storage business. Behind one of the buildings the remains of an old, burnt-down wooden pier projected out into the river, its charred stumps just breaching the waterline. I was getting winded, and hoped that Jimmy would take the road that serviced the warehouses, where he'd be easy to catch up to, or at least shoot at. He kept on through the weeds. I cursed, and he almost trapped himself by running between the buildings, but realized his mistake. He doubled back and went past the far-most building and toward the river. A big black bird perched in a tree screamed at him and flew away as he ran past. I kept on.

The ground along the river was weedy; a stand of spindly trees choked with woody, parasitic vines were rooted near the riverbank and leaned over the scummy water. Insects swarmed.

Another plane went overhead. I couldn't hear anything and stopped running. The clouds parted for a moment; the moon glinted off the water's surface, and I could see that the river took a sharp turn toward my right. Jimmy had run onto a narrow spit of land, effectively corralling himself. I stayed low and moved while the plane whined away. When it was quiet, I stopped and tried to listen. A bug dive-bombed me. I heard a splash in the water and turned that way, but couldn't see much other than the moon's reflection, dancing on the ripples.

I heard movement to my right. He'd suckered me. I spun around and away but still took a punch to the ear. Lights flashed in my head. It rocked me, and I dropped the gun.

Jimmy moved in. I backpedaled as best I could, taking two more punches, both hitting my left shoulder. My arm went numb. I grabbed the trunk of a skinny ailanthus and tried for a kick to Jimmy's knee, but missed. He aimed a punch at my head meant to end this, but my momentum caused me to slip on the wet grass, and his fist sailed past my chin and into the tree trunk; I heard bones snap. He screamed. I jabbed at his eyes with my fingers and made contact, and tried again, for his throat. He flailed, blindly, grabbed me with his broken hand and started hitting me. It was no good. Jimmy had a lousy record in the ring, but he was still a boxer; he'd spent years in the gym, throwing thousands of punches, and I hadn't. I did my best.

There was a *thump.* Jimmy grunted, and fell. Standing behind him was a tall woman, wearing pants and nothing else, holding a length of two-by-four. Her looks were Slavic – thick brow, high cheekbones. Her hair was dark and cut very short. She made to hit Jimmy again, but I held up my hands and said, "No, no. *Nyet* – please." I couldn't tell if she understood me, and held up a finger. "One moment."

The woman nodded and said, *"Ladna.* Oh – Kay." and took a step back. She had trouble moving. She'd lost her shoes, probably in the river. She'd bound her shirt around her right foot as a dressing. It was dark with blood. Her lack of mobility had kept her here, hiding out in the weeds, waiting. She was skinny – small-breasted, and her ribs stood out in the moonlight – but tough-looking. Her torso showed the signs of hiding out in the weeds; she was covered with scratches and insect bites. She held on to the two-by, moving the wood around in her hands to remind me that she had it.

I felt around in the swamp grass and recovered the pistol, and kicked Jimmy in the ribs. "Sit up." He moaned twice, and rolled over and pushed himself up sitting, holding his injured hand to his side, under his arm. His left eye was swollen, and watering badly. I said, "You made yourself some money, moving these people. Why not let it go, now that Pastore's in jail? Why'd you push it?"

"Hey, it wasn't me. I'm just a hired hand –"

"Answer my question."

He thought a second and said, "I didn't want to do no more, honest. That guy – you don't tell that guy no."

"Who? Anton?"

"No. Well, yeah, you didn't fuck with him, neither, but I mean the other."

I pointed toward the van. "You mean Scott, back there?"

He was surprised but said, "Yeah. Him."

"When did he tell you he was your new boss?"

"I don't know, after he come back from Iraq. He said, he'd be making a move and he wanted to keep me on. He said there'd be more money. I didn't care, I was getting tired of dealing with them fucking Hunkies, anyway." He remembered the woman and glanced at her. "I figured I would go with Scott. It didn't seem like there was no other choice, like."

"Take your shoes off, Jimmy. The socks, too."

He didn't like that. "What for?"

He'd been around long enough to know what was going to happen. I didn't want him to shut down on me. I needed him to tell me things, so I encouraged him to hope. "I can't have you following me when I leave. It's either the shoes or I have to do something else." I motioned with the pistol toward his feet. "You cleaned up Pastore's boat with bleach. That's why your shoes are speckled, right?"

"Yeah." He began to undo the laces.

I knew most of this, but I wanted to hear it from him. "Why?"

"We were nervous, me and the guy, the guy driving the boat – "

"The pilot."

"Yeah. We were nervous, with Pastore getting busted, and all. We seen a launch out on the river with warning lights coming our way and figured it for the Coast Guard. We had to get them Hunky broads off the boat. The guy, the pilot, he shown them the gun, but a few of them still wouldn't get in the water. I guess they couldn't swim." He hesitated, looking at the woman with the stick, and said, "You know, it got kinda messy."

"But it wasn't the Coast Guard."

"No. They were fire department guys in that little Boston Whaler they got. They boogied once they heard the gun. How were we supposed to know?" He appealed uselessly to the woman. "You seen it – how could we know?" She stared at him. He turned back to me. "They didn't even come anywheres near us. We come back, later on, you know, in the van, to see if we could pick anybody up." He rubbed at his eye. "Honest."

"Nobody can swim against that current." I pointed at the woman. "This girl was lucky."

Jimmy opened his mouth to say something, but he was at a loss. He gestured helplessly.

I motioned toward his feet with the pistol. He went back to work on the laces. His broken fingers gave him trouble. I said, "After you shot one of them, they all had to go. You didn't count on anybody swimming it to shore, right? You came back to make sure nobody made it. That's what you were doing, here, now."

Jimmy began speaking and stopped a couple times, trying to choose his words and finally said, "Look, most of them got carried away and went under. This one here," he stuck his thumb in the woman's direction, "was going with the current, stroking her way to shore. She's swimming like Johnny fucking Weissmuller, in a Tarzan movie, or something. The guy, the pilot shot at her a couple times. It looked like he hit her, but we couldn't see for sure, and we couldn't follow her in – it gets too shallow around here. The boat would have got stuck." He pulled off one shoe. "By the time we cleaned up the boat it was light out. It's too hairy around here during the day – with the airport and all – all them cops and Homeland Security people. We figured we didn't need to worry about her, she would bleed out or something, but after everything tonight, Scott was paranoid and wanted to make sure." Jimmy looked at the woman and said, "I guess he was right."

"Who's the pilot?"

"I don't know. He's just a guy." I waited and he added, "Honest, he's like you: he never said his name and I never asked it. I'm not stupid."

"What does he look like?" I motioned again with the pistol.

Jimmy went to work on the other shoe and said, "I don't know. He's an old guy. Gray hair. He's medium, like." He rubbed his eye. "I didn't want to hurt you, man. I just got to get clear of all this, you know?" He got his socks off and I pointed to the woman. Jimmy handed her the shoes and socks with his good hand. She unwound the bandage from her foot. The bullet wound looked nasty; it had dug a furrow through the side of her foot from the heel to the little toe. At least it wasn't bleeding anymore. She pulled on a sock, taking care not to re-open the wound.

"Give her your shirt, too." Jimmy didn't like that either, but pulled it off. The woman had gotten the shoes and socks on and stood, pushing herself up with the two-by-four. Jimmy's shirt was too big around for her. She buttoned it and tied the shirt-tails together, under her rib cage.

I said to Jimmy, "How did you get into all this?"

"Them two big guys, them hunkies. They come by the gym a while ago, said they wanted to train. Mostly, they were looking for help."

"And you're always looking for work."

He nodded. "Alls I did was handle them people, you know, on the boat and into the van."

"Why'd you guys kill Reilly?"

"I didn't want no parts of that. That was all Scott – you can ask –" He stopped himself and said, "When Pastore took the bust, Scott said we needed to cover ourselves – make sure there wasn't nothing tying any of us to the boat – Scott said Pastore was always writing stuff down. He said somebody else was taking care of what was in Pastore's house – I guess that was youse – but we had to have a talk with Reilly. Scott found out Reilly was holed up in that house. We just needed to get paperwork, but fucking Scott went crazy – he didn't seem to care about any papers once he started. I couldn't stop him, man, honest."

"What about Joe Dougherty?"

Jimmy looked puzzled. "Who?"

I let it go, and said, "Why did Scott kill George? Why not just pay him to do the job? You know how the cops feel about that – they look hard when one of their own gets killed"

Jimmy shook his head no, and said, "Scott didn't kill him."

"Of course he did. I saw him there."

"No, honest. Nobody wanted to hurt nobody. Scott just wanted the ledger book. He was gonna leave youse two the money."

I chuckled.

"Okay." He made a face and said, "All right. He was gonna take it all."

"Where's my safe?"

Jimmy looked confused. He said, "He never got it."

"I'm losing patience."

"No, look, Scott said it all went to shit, over there at George's shop. He said he seen two people booking out of there, but they lost him. He said he come back around, there's cops all over the place." He rubbed at his eye again and blinked. "Scott picked me up at the gym after that, after you come by. Said he needed help."

"You're not making sense. He didn't call the cops?"

Jimmy looked blank. "Why would Scott call the cops?"

"Okay, Jimmy," I nodded to the woman, "forget about it."

Jimmy said, "Aw, man—" as she swung and stove-in his head. It sounded like a watermelon dropped off a roof.

I stayed out of her reach and said, "Can you speak English?"

She nodded and held her thumb and forefinger about an inch apart. "Small."

"What happened?"

She struggled. "I – come out of water. *Vyrubitsa* – I pass away, here."

"You passed out?" I put my palms together and lay my face across the back of my hand, miming sleep.

She nodded and said, "I passed out," sounding out the words slowly, practicing them.

I had her put down the stick and step back. Jimmy's wallet had a little over a hundred dollars in it, and some ID. His driver's license photo didn't look much like her, but their hair was the same color and length. It was something, and she'd have to make do. I pointed to Jimmy's picture and at her, and back a couple of times, and said, "This is you. Okay?" She seemed to understand. I gave it all to her and motioned her to walk ahead of me. She had a lot of trouble – she was limping badly – but toughed it out.

Scott was sprawled face down alongside the van. I'd hit him in the back, twice. Both rounds hit him high on the left side, through the lung. It looked like either would have done the trick.

I debated with myself for a few moments about dragging him and Jimmy to the river and letting it carry them away, but gave it up. There was no way to connect me with either of them. The woman wasn't up to it, physically, and I wasn't much better off.

I picked up his weapon, a silenced Sig Sauer in .40 caliber and stuck it in my belt, rolled him over and went through his pockets – wallet, keys. He had about two hundred dollars with him.

The inside of the van was mostly empty – some fast-food wrappers and what was left of a roll of duct tape. I showed the woman that the vehicle had an automatic transmission. I said, "Can you drive this?" and made steering motions with my hands. She nodded. I gave her the keys and sketched a map with directions for I-95 North to Allegheny Avenue on a scrap of paper from the door pocket. There were a lot of immigrants from Eastern Europe in that neighborhood. She might find some help there. The best I could do to get this notion across was the Russian word for comrade; I said, "*Tovarich?*" and tapped the map.

She took it, touched her fingertips to her forehead and took them away in a salute. She was tough, and seemed intelligent. She might be able to blend in and disappear. Most people don't really see other people; they only see shadows.

I stuck Scott's wallet in my pocket, walked to the rental car and drove away. I called police dispatch from the road. When the operator came on the line I said, "This is Lieutenant Ruggieri, Major Crimes. Can you play me a 911 call from last night? The one-thousand block of Callowhill Street, at around eight or eight-thirty."

"Sure. Give me a few minutes."

I turned onto the expressway and went over the Platt Memorial Bridge, past the refinery and auto graveyards. The dispatcher came back on when I'd reached 28th Street, "Here you go, Lieutenant."

I listened to the call, and said, "Thank you. Have a good night."

27

Brenda had changed out of the black dress. She opened the door to her apartment wearing a blue silk robe. "Oh. It's you." She let me in but didn't comment on my appearance, just said, "You must be here to give me my share, after all." She was smiling, but didn't really look happy. "Have a seat. I'll get you a drink."

I walked past her into the apartment, and looked at the photographs next to her sofa. "I suppose you were expecting your brother. He won't be coming by." I went into the kitchen. "Dougherty won't either, but you weren't counting on him, anyway."

She was confused but kept it together. She smiled and said, "That's okay. You're here."

"Some guys talk too much. George did."

"George?" Her robe was missing its sash and she busied herself holding it closed. "You're not making any sense."

"Yeah. You know, George Rafferty. I'd forgotten he told me he spoke with you."

"So what?"

"It never was a real problem, before. I suppose the cancer made him careless." She stared like she didn't know what I meant. "He told you how we would do the job."

"What are you talking about?"

I ignored the question and said, "I was already doped when I talked to you at the party." I took the picture of her in the bikini off the refrigerator and showed it to her. "That's why I missed it when you told me you get seasick."

"Look, I would still go out on the boat – wait, how did you – you were in here?" She pulled the robe tighter around her.

"Sure. I'm not George. I did fuck up – I should have figured it out earlier, when I saw your brother's picture in here. He was an M.P.

Military Police have to qualify with the pistol. I'll bet Scotty shot expert." She stood mute. "It was your deal all along. You brought your brother in to take over from Anton, but you ran everything, right?" I took a step toward her.

She backed up until she bumped against the Kitchen Aid on the counter, and nodded.

"You saw Marcolina and me at the party tonight – saw us come into the house before we saw you – and you sent a text to Anton. If either of us hurt the other, it would only be good for you. You sent one to Scott, too."

She composed herself and said, "Look, there's money in this for you."

"There is no money in that safe, wherever it is. You and your brother Scott were cutting Pastore and Anton out of the business."

She began to speak, but stopped.

I said, "Two nights ago, your guys dumped that load of people in the river."

She pointed toward the living room. "I've got money here. I can make this right."

"The money in your file cabinet? I already took that." I patted my pocket. "I'm a thief."

"No, not that. I've got real money – I've got it stashed in the bathroom, behind the backsplash." She pointed again, more insistently.

I glanced in that direction. When I looked back she was fixing her robe again. I said, "What does Pastore have that you want?"

She began to speak, stopped and composed herself and said, "Vic had a cash flow problem this past fall and it worried him. He signed his boat over to me a few months ago – he was afraid he'd lose it. He made me sign a post-dated bill of sale selling it back to him for a dollar."

"All this was over a boat?"

"That boat is perfect for what we do. Nobody would suspect that it was anything but a rich guy's toy. I could never replace it on my own. It costs three million dollars. Without it, we're pretty much out of business. Look," she took a step toward me. Her left hand was caught up in the folds of her robe. "Look, we can work this out.

I've made a lot of money in this business." I looked behind her, at the counter. Shiny black handles stood proud of the wooden knife block. A paring knife slot was empty. "We can make a lot more – you and me." She let the front of her robe fall open. She was naked underneath. "This could be really good."

I dragged the Sig from my waistband, pressed the muzzle between her breasts and fired. Even silenced, it sounded loud. She dropped there, her fingers still clutching the paring knife. I wiped it off and slid it back into the block. I wiped down the Sig, unscrewed the silencer and pressed the gun into her hand, pushing her left thumb through the trigger guard.

She was pretty enough for investigators to buy the bullet through the heart. She wouldn't want a closed casket.

There was no money behind the backsplash in the bathroom. Her being left-handed would make this next part difficult. I studied her handwriting in the essays from the composition books and her journal. I can do three or four different styles of handwriting, but none close enough to hers to fool an expert. Tougher than that would be copying her prose style. She wrote well, and a lot of people, like the judge, knew her writing. I crafted a suicide note, trying to mimic the tone of her journal entries – I used her line about 'getting to the end of someone' – and redid the note four times until I was satisfied. I put it on the counter, took the copies with me, locked her door, and left.

28

I picked up Reilly's bag from Thirtieth Street Station. The sun was coming up as I parked the car in the Nine Hundred block of Callowhill Street. Rainwater puddled in the gutter at 10th, the drain clogged with debris. I walked around to the street behind George's shop. From inside I heard the whine of an electric drill; it drowned out the small noises I made raising the back window. George's car was still there.

I climbed inside quietly. On the far side of the building, at the bench, two people worked by the light of a gooseneck lamp, one hunched over, leaning his weight onto the drill that he held, two-handed. A wisp of smoke curled up from the work. I could smell the drill motor overheating. It was the safe he labored over, the lengths of two by six framing still bolted to its sides. Two bicycles stood idle, alongside the far wall. I crept forward and crouched, behind the car. I recognized the two. They were the hipster couple that had pedaled past me the previous night, right around the corner from here.

The girl flipped her long, black hair behind her and spoke to be heard over the drill. "It shouldn't be taking this long, should it?" When the boy didn't respond, she said more loudly, "Why's it taking so long?" She took off her cat's-eye glasses and cleaned them on her shirt.

The boy stopped drilling and stood up straight, stretching. "The metal is tough." He had taken off his flannel shirt and tied its sleeves around his waist. There were sweat stains under the arms of his light blue T-shirt. A small pistol lay on the bench near him.

"This is taking longer than I thought it would." She was faced away from me, and I could see tattooed skin in the gap between her shirt and pants, and the straps of her thong.

The kid was annoyed. "It's a safe. It's supposed to be hard." The girl stayed quiet. The boy took a chuck key and removed the bit, and replaced it with another from an old drill index on the bench. "All of these are pretty dull. We might have to go someplace and buy more bits."

"I'll go. Write down what I should get. I'll pick up something to eat, too. I'm hungry."

I dragged the Glock free and stepped out from behind the car. "Hey."

The girl screamed. They both turned toward me. I said, "You need to run some oil along the bit while you drill. That keeps it from burning out. George Rafferty could have told you that."

The boy reached for his gun. The girl screamed, "No, don't," as I shot him. She stood there, transfixed, staring at the boy on the floor, and looked back up at me. "Please, don't shoot me, mister." Her voice cracked and she started to cry. "Please – I – I'll suck your dick." A dark stain spread down the crotch of her jeans.

"Have a seat." I nodded toward a chair, away from the boy and his gun. "I'm not going to hurt you." She hesitated. I pointed to the dead kid and said, "He didn't give me any choice. Go on, sit down." When she did, I moved along with her, in an arc, around the kid on the floor, to stand by the bench. I said, "George did work on your guitars and amplifiers. That's how you knew him, right?" The girl nodded. "Tell me the rest." I stuck the kid's pistol into my waistband.

She was having trouble, but said, "I didn't want to hurt him. That was James – he said Mister Rafferty was dying anyway. I just wanted –"

I didn't need any of that. "How did you know about this?" I tapped the safe with the butt of the Glock.

She shifted in the seat. "James was learning about amplifiers and stuff from Mr. Rafferty." She looked down at her wet pants. "He likes to talk about things," she sobbed and choked out, "you know?"

I nodded. "Yeah, I know. How did you get in here?"

"James unlocked the back window while he was here, yesterday. We climbed in after Mr. Rafferty left last night."

"Where did you hide the safe?"

She pointed. "Underneath his car. James had wanted to move it to the practice hall, but then he saw a guy in a van parked down the street and got freaked out. I said the cops would never look under the car, and they'd be done here in a few hours and that way we could come back and use Mr. Rafferty's tools." She tugged at the fabric of her wet pant legs.

I nodded. "And you're the one who called the police?"

She hesitated, and said, "Yeah." She was getting upset again.

"What were you going to do with the money?"

She bit her lip and said, "We were going to move to L.A. That's where the business is. There's no real music scene in Philadelphia, not really, and –" She started crying again.

I said, "Shh. It's all right." Streaks of black eye makeup ran down her cheeks. "Here," I tossed her my handkerchief, "clean your face."

She said, 'Thanks." She took off her glasses, and as she wiped her eyes, I shot her.

I pulled the handkerchief out of her hands and pushed it into my back pocket. I threw the kid's gun into a trashcan under the bench and looked at the safe. The kid hadn't known what he was doing. Its face was made of hardened steel. I flipped it over and drilled holes in its back, describing the corners of a rough, four by eight inch rectangle, beginning with a quarter-inch bit, moving up to three-eighths, and finally half-inch, trickling oil along the bit through the entire operation, until the holes were big enough to accommodate a Sawzall blade. I cut from hole to hole, changing blades as needed, and when I finished the final run, the square piece of metal fell inside the box. I was sweating. I wiped my face with the handkerchief. I could smell the girl on it.

I took away the metal waste, reached back inside the box and pulled out its contents. There was no money, just sheaths of paper – contracts, receipts – anything to document other's involvement in Pastore's criminal enterprises. There was even the signed, post-dated bill of sale for the boat, from Brenda back to Pastore. I turned off the lights left andput all the paperwork in Reilly's bag. I shut the trunk and drove across the Ben Franklin Bridge into Jersey.

29

"The heat wave is expected to continue through the weekend, with temperatures in the high eighties." The neighborhood I drove through wasn't far from the bridge. It had been built as naval officer housing during WWII. The radio announcer continued, "In local news, federal investigators, along with local and state police entered the home of State Senator Victor Pastore this morning. Senator Pastore is currently in federal custody, awaiting arraignment. SEPTA officials now say it may take up to four months before its regional rail lines can be restored to full service – "

I parked the rental two blocks away and approached the address from the opposite side of the block. The homes here were similar in materials, but varied in style. There were half a dozen or so basic designs that repeated at intervals. They were nice. Through the yards, I recognized the back of the house from the one time I'd been there. It was a two-story bungalow. There was a small patio in the back, with a charcoal grill and lawn furniture. I kept an eye on the windows as I hopped the fence and stepped across the wet grass to the back entrance. A screen door revealed an empty kitchen. I tried the handle. It was locked.

I looked around. There was a blackened spatula on a table next to the grill. I took it and slid the blade between the door and the jam and worked open the latch, dragged the Glock from my waistband and pulled open the screen door.

Inside it was dim. I stood there for a few moments and let myself adjust to the quiet of the house. The kitchen was clean – everything put away. It had a sense of finality, but I could smell fresh coffee.

A black suitcase sat on the dining room table. Past the living room, I could see through the front picture window. The front door was ajar. Through the screen door I could hear birds chirping.

A toilet flushed upstairs. A minute later, Tom came down the steps, carrying a mug. He was startled when he saw me, but only said, "Hi," and took a sip of his coffee.

"Taking a trip?"

"Yeah, Maine. I need a vacation. This weather's already getting to me." He glanced at the weapon in my hand. "I told Pete to take care of the bar."

"He'll deal with the broken cooler?"

"Yeah."

"You flying?"

"Yeah. I called for a cab to take me to the airport. I hate to deal with the parking there, you know?" He looked toward the street. "Should be here soon."

"Sit down a minute."

He took a seat at the dining room table.

"Those weren't Ritalin you sold me."

"I didn't know what those guys had planned. I didn't want you hurt – I never wanted anybody hurt – there was no need." He gestured pointlessly and continued, "I figured if you got doped up you'd pass out somewhere and that would be that. I know none of that matters, I just, you know, I want you to know."

"You called the police when you heard from Flipper."

Tom started to say something but stopped and just said, "Yeah."

"You got this whole thing started, right? While you were still on the job?"

"Yeah, I worked the river my last few years in the department. I met some guys down at the port. You know, you talk. It was easy money. Then Pastore had some trouble last fall. He let us use his boat." He waited for me to say something, and continued, "I was trying to help those people. Most of them are coming from terrible places, and this is their only way here." He stared at me and said, "I'll give you the cash I've got on me," and made to open the suitcase.

I brought the pistol up.

Tom held his hands out. "I don't have a gun in there. You can't take a gun on a plane."

I said, "Your cab's here," and shot him as he turned to look out at the empty street.

There was a little automatic in the suitcase side pocket. He must have planned to throw it away once he got to the airport. When the cab did pull up, I apologized and told the driver I didn't need the ride after all. I tipped him with the last of Dougherty's twenties.

Tom had two hundred dollars in twenties in his wallet. I dragged him to the basement door, pushed him down the steps, and set the central air to fifty-five degrees. There were six thousand dollars in hundreds in the lining of Tom's suitcase. I spent forty minutes searching the house but didn't find any more money.

I realized that George had been right about that first guy he'd called. Whoever he was, he hadn't had any part in this. George had been right about almost everything.

It had been a long night. It hadn't been profitable but I'd made a point: it didn't pay to mess with my partners or me.

I walked back to the rental car. Before I got inside, I bent down to tie my shoe and dropped the Glock and the box of cartridges into a sewer inlet on the corner.

*

Jerry was rolling down the awning in front of Men's Finest when I pulled up. He said, "Hey, it's the sensible guy."

I put Reilly's bag on the pavement and said, "Inside are the things your friend wanted."

"I'll see to it that he gets them." He picked up the bag and said, "Can I interest you in anything?"

"No thanks. Not today."

*

Susan kissed me and said, "You never came home for the money."

"I didn't need it. I'll put it back in the wall tomorrow."

"You look wiped out. Do you want something to eat?"

"Later. I need a shower and sleep, first."

She nodded and said, "Sure." She let me go and said, "Was there much?"

"I'll count it later. Some goes to a guy, and I have to get another car." I kissed her again and moved toward the stairs. "It's likely a wash."

"After all that? You must be disappointed."

I nodded and went upstairs. I took off my clothes as the water in the shower warmed.

About the Author

Tony Knighton is a Lieutenant in the Philadelphia Fire Department, a twenty-nine year veteran.

He has published short fiction in Static Movement Online and Dark Reveries.

"The Scavengers" was previously published in the anthology *Shocklines: Fresh Voices in Terror* from Cemetery Dance Publications. "Sunrise" originally appeared in the anthology *Equilibrium Overturned* from Grey Matter Press.

Tony's first book, a collection of short stories titled *Happy Hour and Other Philadelphia Cruelties*, was published by Crime Wave Press in 2015.

Word-of-mouth is essential for any author to succeed.
If you enjoyed *Three Hours Past Midnight*, please consider leaving a review on Amazon.
Even a couple of lines would make a difference and would be extremely appreciated.

Crime Wave Press is a Hong Kong based fiction imprint that endeavors to publish the best new crime novels from around the globe.

Founded in 2012 by acclaimed publisher Hans Kemp of Visionary World and seasoned writer Tom Vater, **Crime Wave Press** publishes a range of crime fiction – from whodunits to Noir and Hardboiled, from historical mysteries to espionage thrillers, from literary crime to pulp fiction, from highly commercial page turners to marginal texts exploring the world's dark underbelly.

Crime Wave Press promotes strong voices, exceptional talent and unique points of view in the crime fiction genre.

Visit our website: www.crimewavepress.com
Follow us on Facebook: www.facebook.com/CrimeWavePress

If you like to be among the first to hear about new **Crime Wave Press** releases and special **Crime Wave Press** promotions sign up for our mailing list here.
We promise to never share your email with anyone.
The **Crime Wave Press** Team

Made in the USA
Lexington, KY
19 June 2018